CONIUM

REVIEW

vol. 9

J—
Thanks for your
support — and for keeping
my cabinets stocked
with cool mugs.
[signature]

Conium Press
Portland, OR

The Conium Review
Vol. 9
© 2020 Conium Press
Portland, OR

http://www.coniumreview.com

ISBN-13 978-1-942387-16-9
ISSN 2164-6252

Cover Image: © LoveTheWind / licensed through iStock
Layout & Design: James R. Gapinski

[contents]

THE HUSBANDS

Heather Cripps

THE HUSBANDS

Heather Cripps

I'm staring out the window at the house across the street, and I'm starting to make some connections. I'm standing in the kitchen, and Husband is next to me on his knees, hands in the cupboard, looking for some Tupperware. I nearly say it out loud, "I'm starting to make some connections," but I don't.

I'm going to break into that house today. I don't even nearly say this out loud, instead when Husband looks up, frowning at me for losing the plastic tub the right size for his sandwich, I take the thought and hide it deeper inside myself.

"I'm going to have to buy a sandwich on the way to work," he says, "in one of those plastic triangles. Terrible for the environment."

I don't reply. I take a sip of my coffee and watch the house. A child cycles by. There is a breeze. The curtain in the front room moves a little. I think.

Husband stares at the side of my head, sighs, and then goes to get his coat.

"You can eat that sandwich," he says, and points to an unsliced cheese and salad on the chopping board. Then he leaves. I won't. I won't eat the sandwich.

Husband drives away; I watch him go, watch his license plate until I can't read it anymore. Then I go to the table where there are the newspaper clippings of a few things, articles about some people in the general area who have gone missing. One of them is a report of a rogue husband reappearing in the woods at night. People in the neighbourhood spotted him: teenagers messing around there, new wives on a late-night run, old wives on a just-need-to-get-out-the-house walk.

"I saw him, I'm not crazy," a teenager is a quoted in the newspaper, "He was wearing a white t shirt and jeans and his eyes looked like he was dead and he didn't answer us when we called, didn't understand what we were saying. He had his hands in the river, and no shoes on."

I've been reading all this news for a while, making connections. I wait until ten which is when the neighbor leaves to go to the community centre for Yoga. Five wives and a husband leave at the same time to go to the same yoga session.

The neighbor moved here fifteen years ago, around when I first got married to Husband, when we were happy. The neighbor is single and has no children. When she moved in, another neighbor said, "Shame. This is a family place."

I put my coat on and go over the road. Our street is tidy and neat, with identical shaped patches of grass, one each, outside of the houses, always mown and trimmed. No one drops litter, no one's dog mess is left behind, no one paints their house bright pink or throws toilet paper or eggs on Halloween. The only drawback to living here is that people occasionally go missing. The worst: a small boy whose family couldn't take it and moved away; the best: Angry Husband, whose wife always wore sunglasses.

I knock on the door to the house across the road, and then when there is no answer, I try the door and it opens so I go inside. Everyone else locks their door, she hasn't, these are the connections.

The woman who lives here looks like everyone else. She fits in. She wears a grey cardigan. She smiles at the supermarket clerk. She tips the waiters. She mows her lawn or asks a neighbourhood husband to do it for her. I see her at church. But she doesn't close her eyes when she prays and once when she was saying her Our Father, she was looking straight at me.

Inside her house is cream carpets and clean surfaces and a nice painting of a forest. There are DVDs and books stacked on shelves in her den and a big flat screen TV. There are framed photos of children and a wedding where she is not the bride.

I find what I am looking for in the cupboard under her kitchen sink. Glass bottles, wine size, sheer. Bottles and bottles of missing people. They are shrunk and silent, eyes closed, skin shrivelled. There are people I recognise, the boy and Angry Husband, and people I don't. There is the groom from the picture in which she is not the bride. I pick up this groom and shake him. He looks too big to have fit through the neck of the bottle. But there he is. The next bottle I pick up is empty but still lives in the cupboard.

The front door closes, and the woman finds me, on my hands and knees, hands in the cupboard. Maybe yoga was cancelled or maybe she knew I was coming or maybe an hour has passed already. I get up and smooth my skirt. I'm still holding the empty bottle.

"I let that one go," the neighbor says. "I felt bad for the wife. She actually loved him."

I must look frightened because she says, "I don't do women," and lets me pass her and go home.

I read the papers I have saved again and then rip them up, shoving them in the bottom of the rubbish bag and then take the bag out to the yard. I go back to the window and look at the house. Then I can't look at it. Then I can again. A fly sits on the cheese and salad sandwich and I swat it away.

Husband comes home. I've made him his favorite dinner, cracked open a bottle of wine. When I get up to take his plate, I kiss the top of his head, and ask him to take the bottle over the road to the neighbour.

"She's recycling them," I say, and he looks up at me like we might just be happy again.

VIVARIUM

Miranda Williams

VIVARIUM

Miranda Williams

The day you began speaking to plants, Mom called me. It was one of those bloody days where the sunset coughed red into the clouds. I held the phone between cheek and shoulder but did nothing with my hands. Her voice was light and crisp like an apple slice, and she made her phone calls sound common, though we both knew they weren't.

"Won't you come over for dinner, Colin?" She said my name after every sentence. I could picture her rolling the seam of her dress between her fingers like she did.

"It's already six. I was probably going to do some work things or read," I said.

Usually around that time, I liked to pace in my bathroom, in front of the full panel mirror. Still in my work suit, sometimes I did it with a glass of wine. Glanced at myself. Smiled. With teeth. Without.

Mom sighed. "It's Mary, Colin. She's not well."

Not well. I thought I'd be able to feel it when you were sick. Perhaps we traded something in the womb, a lung or a hand, so we always knew each other.

"What happened? Is she okay?"

"She's always been unique, I know that. She had that bug phase when she was little." I heard the crinkle of her breath. The words pained her. "But, I'm worried she's far gone, Colin. I never thought she'd be the one to—"

She snipped her words. I didn't mind—you've always been her favorite. She loved you like a daughter and me like her daughter's brother. You understood this, too. To make it up to me, you'd hang my drawings on your bedroom wall and slide the last tofu dumpling on my plate when we got takeout.

"Of course. I'll be there in thirty minutes or so."

"Thank you, Colin. You'll see. She might as well be howling to the moon."

. . .

In middle school, you took to the habit of lying on your back in the sand, limbs all spread like a blooming flower and waiting for it to rain. With your grey eyes fixed on the dark clouds, it seemed you were a part of them; the shadows turned you green. It only happened after holidays, or piano recitals, or slumber parties with friends. Mom and I watched you from the kitchen window, peeking through sprouts of cilantro and basil leaves lining the sill. She sighed and said you were a deep soul.

"What do you think she is trying to do?" I asked.

"Mary has a lot to think about," she said, pressing her red-stained lips together until there was nothing but a line. I did the same. "Sometimes, when it feels like I'm drowning, Mary carries me. She carries us."

I nodded vigorously, as if I couldn't agree more. Our kitchen smelled of lemon cleaner and over-ripe tomatoes; it always did. We loved it that way. Mom crouched to get a baking sheet, but I couldn't stop looking at you. The first droplets of rain fell. You didn't even blink. Even as the sand softened and splashed. I wondered if it hurt you.

"Do you think I could carry us too, Mom? Do I carry Mary?"

I met eyes. Her forehead shriveled with wrinkles. When she brushed the hair away from my forehead, her fingers felt cold and squashed, like the long tubes of yogurt we ate for breakfast.

"I think you're more like an anchor, Dear. If Mary keeps us afloat, I think you make sure we don't drift too far," she said.

I blinked up at her and nodded again. We both paused. "I think you could be the flag, Mom."

I didn't know what that meant. She laughed like one does when they can no longer speak and continued with her baking sheet.

The sky could have mauled you. Chewed until your body turned into a mush of sunlight and wispy clouds. You let the rain slap until it relented to a light kiss. Eventually, with the warmth of the oven and the baked eggplant wafting, you came inside, water puddling on the linoleum. The yellow smiley face on your shirt had darkened to a light brown.

Mom gasped quietly. "Love, your hair is all muddy. Let's go upstairs, and I'll wash it out." She wished to pretend this was new each time, that you were a mysterious force. Something tangled in my stomach, then.

"I can do it," I said. "I want to help, Mom. You're finishing dinner."

The smile drained from her lips and eyes. "Okay, Colin. If you're sure."

"I am. We'll be right back down to eat."

She nodded, frown still budding, and ripped open a plastic package of spinach.

I rinsed you in Mom's bathtub. A blanket of hot water covered our feet and reached for the cuffs of my jeans. The shower curtain gummed to the wall with a line of suction cups. It was dark blue and then light blue and then white. With the yellowy dim lights, it was like we were at the ocean. We'd never been to one before.

I sifted the sand from your hair with a brush. The shower was hot. Rainforest temperature. It made everything stick to you—hair slicked, jeans a wrinkled second skin snaking your legs. You reminded me of stick-bug. All twigs and bulbs. Small. Squashable.

Sometimes, I wanted to make you even smaller. Prove to myself you were real. Human. Nothing more than I. A boat can have holes, I thought, clenching my jaw. On the next brush, I pulled harder. A flinch, but you said nothing. The steam turned my nose runny. Guilt wilted me for the rest of the night.

When the sand had all left your hair, collecting at the drain in a spider web of pebbles and flecks of beige, you turned the water off. Turned. Face shiny and pink like an unripe watermelon.

"Thanks, Colin," you said.

Your steps plotted dark wet patches into the carpet. They trailed the house like breadcrumbs. A path back to you in case we got lost.

. . .

I arrived at your house—a large square thing with reddish wood flooring and spongy beige couches—and you were crisscrossed in the living room, planted in a circle of book stacks, empty water glasses, and a wispy bonsai tree stuffed into a fishbowl. Its extended roots pressed to glass like a hand. You had chopped your hair off. It fluttered around your chin as you buzzed between books. Mom said you were working, as usual. She had three veggie burgers thawing on the counter. The color of canned tuna. One time, when we both went to college, I sat in my car and ate five McDonald's double cheeseburgers just to tell Mom after. With oily fingertips, I finished crumpling the last yellow paper and dialed her number.

"I eat meat now," I said, when she answered. The salty aftertaste of beef and pickles crawled over my smile. I was ready for war, but she was calm.

"I don't know why you would want that, Colin."

She said it like I had told her I wanted to pick up a new hobby—basketball or magic tricks. The burgers sat piled in my stomach. Bloating. Threatening to topple over. Mom didn't say anything else, and I drove to our apartment while the air conditioner spat the scent of grease. After throwing my keys and wallet on the counter, hearing their clang on the granite, I vomited into the kitchen sink. Blue Powerade and soggy bread lumps. You poured me a glass of water.

"Rough day?" You had asked me.

I thought about asking you the same question then, watching the jittered movements of your fingers. Mom spoke.

"Just try to figure out what's wrong. I've done all I can."

I turned to her, but it was you she was looking at. Bulging, red-rimmed eyes and stiff, hair-sprayed curls. She nodded when she met my gaze. Coming there was worth it for that second. Mom left for the kitchen, and feet thumped as I stepped out of the entryway. For some reason, I thought you wouldn't notice my arrival, but you sprung up from the ground when you saw. So thin and tall. Your smile revealed perfectly square teeth like saltine crackers. We hugged, both chilled from sweat.

"Haven't seen you since Christmas," I said. It was May. You had invited me over New Year's too, but I couldn't bring myself to say yes. An office party—tiny glasses of gin with speared olives, expensive watches, and waxy talks about children and spouses—was the lie I told.

"I know." You kept your smile. Toothy and rose-cheeked. I smiled too. "I always miss having a twin." There was a pause. Ceiling fan cooing. Veggie burgers hissing. Inhale. Exhale. "Did Mom ask you to come here? I figured she would soon."

My grin slipped, but you didn't seem to mind. Your living room smelled saccharin. Vanilla candles and dishes of sugar-free caramels. "I think she's worried, Mary."

My sight drifted to the bonsai tree. Leaves oval like fingernails. Its ashy trunk was fat and covered in wrinkles. Reminded me of an old secluded shaman witch, ready to turn me into a frog. You held my shoulder, rubbing the polyester covering it with your thumb.

"She shouldn't be," you said, looking towards the bonsai too. "At first, new things seem strange. But, once they're done, you'll wonder why it hadn't always been that way."

With a slight sheen, your forehead reflected the light. A tiny rippling sun. You felt alien in that moment. Insectile. Speaking in chirps. Unreachable under a dark-plated carapace. I hated how certain you were. Everything was controlled. You'd always been that way.

"Something is wrong. Mom wants me to help," I said,

stepping out of your touch. Doing so made me want to cry. Your eyes, it seemed, didn't have the bruisy circles they once possessed, but the irises were still pale and silver and too-big.

"It's okay, Colin," you mothered, stepping closer. "I feel like I can breathe now. That's all."

I nodded, not knowing what else was necessary. You never ceased smiling. Both warmth and bitterness dripped from me. Merged with my sweat. Mom called from the kitchen, and, as we left the living room, I thought of the bonsai. Its root hand against the glass. Scratching at it. Begging to be let out.

. . .

You quit your job, just left your boss a voicemail, Mom told us at the table, as if you were also unaware of this fact. We sat like a triangle: a shiny squarish stool between us with Mom parallel to it. Three lights with round, red shades dangled from the ceiling, spraying the kitchen in flesh color. You seemed pained—bunched eyebrows and white knuckles—separating your burger into cubes with a fork. I chewed slowly, forcing the mush back and forth with my tongue, grinding it with canines, before swallowing. The guilt—the understanding that you would defend me—caused me to speak.

"I am sure Mary can find another job whenever she wants. Any lab would be lucky to have her," I said.

We were all silent for a second. Another. Me and Mom both looked at you. I tried to send a telepathic message, in the way twins should be able too. I didn't know the exact words. Something like: *smile, nod, be with me, help me.* But you heard nothing. You continued slicing at the food. Sharp, meticulous cuts like a surgeon. The placemat shifted with your plate as if it were your flinching, cloth-skinned patient. Mom's stare darted to me. She pouted her lips in the angry way she did, but her quivering told me she only wanted to cry. Her food was untouched. The lettuce on my burger was clammy: too dark in color, soft, and nearly undetected under the thick slabs of tomato. I took another bite, and Mom raised an eyebrow. *Do you see now?* She asked.

We spent the rest of dinner silent. The sprinklers ticked outside, and your knife skidded along the glazed porcelain. We both finished before you. Only a few pieces missing from your butcher of hamburger bun and vegetables, yet you still told Mom dinner was great. Thank you. She was relieved: smile, squeezed handhold, you're welcome.

"I better get going," I said, standing from the table. "Have to go into work early."

You hugged me again at the front door before I left. We stood half inside and half out. Breath hot, panting on my neck, like you'd just been running, you said, "I love you."

.　.　.

Driving home, the earth argued with me. I hit every bump in the road. Wind cracked through my window in a screech. The sky was a mess of blacks and blues like an oil spill. I didn't like listening to music in the car. Neither did you. I let bubbly pop rattle anyways.

When we all still lived together—before you bought a big house, and I moved out, and Mom sold our withered ranch-style place at the end of a sandy cul-de-sac—you two had a routine at night. Ritual. Sacred. I felt wrong for witnessing it even once.

Two glasses of water with the thin severed limb of a lemon floating in each. You took them to her bedroom on a glass, flower-printed serving dish. Freshly showered, your hair was wound into a shiny bun and the cuffs of pajama pants covered your feet, so you slid like a ghost. Mom would be in her nightgown. Always silk and elegant. Makeup scrubbed away to clear smoothness. She always cried when the sun left. We knew from her eyes. All three of ours were the same. Her body would be straight and stiff on her bed, arms crossed over like a dead person's, and you'd sit on the other side. On the lacy pink pillows, near her face. Then, you'd kiss your fingertips, press them to the tops of her cheeks so the wrinkles in her forehead would disappear. She'd cover your hands with hers. A stack of skin. Thank you, Love. Everything grows, Mom.

The radio was garbled static. I drove over a speed bump. Not slowing at all. Everything grows.

.   .   .

In a week, Mom called me again. You moved into the greenhouse, she said. Took nothing. Not even the books. I told her I'd be over soon.

The kitchen in my apartment existed like a museum — immaculate and polished, a shelf with knick-knacks and coffee mugs and wine glasses, dish towels that matched the oven mitts, racks of spices with the labels all facing forward, a few framed signs with blocky lettering. Let's eat. Welcome, they said. I kept my sink empty.

I sat at my table — circular, cherry wood, five-seater. The candle in the center was pine. My hope was people would think I liked hiking. Smoke swirled where it burned. Keeping you waiting was necessary. I'm sorry. After thirty minutes or forty, I blew out the flame and went to your house. Mom let me in before I could even knock.

"Colin, it's much worse than it was. She won't eat. She won't leave the greenhouse. I don't know what she's doing," she said, nervous, picking at a loose thread on her dress. A fleck of red lipstick stuck to her teeth. Though I hated it, there was a slight excitement in seeing her so worried. You wouldn't have felt that.

"I'll talk to her, Mom. I'm sure she's fine," I said, holding her shoulder, rubbing in circles like you would. "I'm going to go check on her."

Something writhed in my stomach as I stepped toward the glass door. Something bloody or drowning, swarmed by lungs, intestines, tissue. Its rot swirled up my throat. I slid the door open anyways. Humidity stuck to everything: the two oak trees sunk with exhaust, grass yellow and parched. The greenhouse curved over a village of vegetables, shrubs, and succulents. A cloudy glass cylinder. The door was cracked open, and flies zipped in and out like they were lost. Stepping into the yard, I squinted. It wasn't too bright, but I felt it should be. Cicadas rattled. A drumroll to my arrival. The dead ground crinkled under my feet and, entering, I didn't see you. There were two plots to each side. Cherry tomatoes, Romas, and chili peppers that boiled from the green like bug bites. Zucchini and summer squash choked in soil. Giant plantain lilies. Rosemary. The slithering bodies of vines and leaves rose nearly to the ceiling and in between sat a long table clustered with potted things.

"Mary," I whispered. It seemed important to whisper.

You didn't respond.

I tip-toed next to the table's edge, brushing the bladed ends of cacti, soil-dusted ceramic, and wet mist with my fingertips. You felt predator in that moment: watching, silent, deadly. Ready for you to jump out with new fangs or claws. My pulse battered like a rabbit's. I sped my pace and found you in seconds. Curled like a baby bird. Still an embryo. Eyes closed. Shaded under the weeping figs and monstera in only underwear. Your skin was a muted green—lighter than the grass beneath you—and your limbs were skeletal with round, protruding knobs for joints.

"Mary," I repeated, plummeting to my knees. "Are you okay, Mary?"

I shook your arm; your skin was too cold for the warmth of the day. Squashy like gelatin. Like your skin would burst. I took my hand away, suddenly aware of my sweat and my breath and the buzzing of the bugs, the plants, the heat. But you opened your eyes. Slow and controlled like you hadn't even been asleep. You tilted your head up, facing me, keeping the rest of your body shelled. The color had melted from your irises—nearly white—and your hair was all plastered like a spider web on your neck and cheeks. You smiled. Wide. Full of teeth and eyebrows like mine. I could picture it on myself. Could mimic it. It would be like we were toddlers pushing each other on swing sets and kicking up sand.

"Colin," you said, "you're here."

Your words were long and syrupy. I sat on my heels, careful not to touch you.

"You're dying," I said. My throat closed like it was being stuffed with dirt. I wondered if it was possible to bury someone from the inside-out. Shaking your head as if swaying, the smile remained. You were always smiling, it seemed.

"Not dying, Colin. Growing. I am evolving into what I was meant to be," You gazed up at a lofty fern plant hung over us.

"Mom says you're not healthy. You need to come inside," I told you. We both knew it would serve no purpose.

You hummed for a moment. Contemplative or meditating. Everything was so slow, so languid. It would sedate until there was no movement at all. "Mom will come to accept it. She knows my purpose more than anyone."

"What are you talking about, Mary?" I wanted to plunge my fingers into the ground and rip it to pieces.

"It's so simple. I am here for others. I am here to give. Like them," you said, circling your neck. "I was never meant to exist this way."

I imagined sitting with Mom during the next holiday — kitchen table rimmed with polished silverware, a pile of envelopes with gift cards, her expensive perfume — without you there. Without your calm. It made my eyes sting.

"You sound insane. Crazy. You need help. What is happening?" I asked. A fly landed on your nose before quickly taking flight again.

"I am going to be with them. I'm going to bloom. It's the way it was always going to be."

"You need to come inside."

"I can't."

"Mary, why are you doing this?" I said. The veins in your arms, I noticed, bulged. All thick, emerald, and branched. Your mouth finally returned flat.

"I must," was all you said.

I stood. My dark jeans were stained a muddy color. When I turned to go back inside, I thought of you leaping from your cocoon. Coming after me. Like you would have if we were younger. But, you didn't. You stayed.

At the greenhouse entrance, I stopped. The plants were everywhere. A family. A city. A world. Closest to me was a potted Fittonia: a body of leaves shoved into a sheeny red bowl etched with hearts. Her leaves—large and flame-shaped and striped—were green but also pink. A skin tone. Light, like the corners of eyes.

Before I left, I grabbed the pot's edge and sent it to the ground. Killed it. I thought it would shatter, but it only thumped. The soil, freckled with eggshells, spilt over the grass. Bled over the stems and leaves. I thought of you mourning over her, your new kind, once I was gone. Then, I imagined your tears putting her back together again. The soil recollecting. The bowl clean and new. The vines springing up and reaching to the other vegetation. I am here, she would say. I am here.

· · ·

I found Mom pacing in the living room. Bunching and releasing the side of her dress like a massage therapist. Burgundy wasn't a good color on her. When she looked up, there was a drizzle of hope. It left when she saw I'd returned alone.

"She's stubborn, Mom. We'll get her back, though," I said, teetering at the entry wall. Far enough from touch. My skin itched.

Mom looked down and then up again, took two more steps, clenched the dress. "I need you to do this, Colin."

I rolled her words in my mouth. Moved my tongue to form them just to feel their shape. *I need you.*

That night, dinner was a pimple, a boil. Something waiting to burst. Hived under a cherry haze, we both moved in quick darts. We drank red wine from antique madeira glasses because it felt like the end, drained spoonfuls of quinoa soup, and stared hard at the salt and pepper shakers. Sitting at opposite heads of the table put us worlds apart. Mom was not going to speak to me. You would have asked a question. *How is it on that side of town? Do you like your apartment? What did you do this weekend?*

I sucked up my last bite of soup and met eyes with her forehead wrinkles and long, scant nose. She stared at her soup, stirring too fast. A tornado in a bowl.

"I got a promotion at work," I said.

I didn't.

Mom looked up. Lifted eyebrows. A smile like a worm across her face and a swallow. She went back to stirring the soup.

###

I'll stay to watch over you, I told Mom. I can sleep on the couch. She nodded, pleased. Her figure turned into a wispy shadowed sliver as she drifted down the hall. The electric clock on the bookshelf blinked at me. I spent thirty minutes sinking my fists into the couch's firm cushions. They were the same color as our skin— we both could have faded into it like a chameleon. Then, I went back to the greenhouse. The moon dangled over it. Full and pure white. The Fittonia was still ragged and twisting, now drowned in night sky, and you were the same as when I left.

"Mary," I whispered again and again, sitting on the grass. But you didn't speak. Didn't move. It was the first time you were quiet with me. The first time you let me go. You were blue and shimmery now. I imagined, for a moment, what it would feel like to drown. The ocean would pour into me, drag into the abyss, until I laid sprawled on the seabed with only crustaceans and seaweed. This wasn't a drowning, but a baptism.

I looked up at the greenhouse ceiling. The moon was hole in the sky, dripping with blinding but beautiful light. I kissed my fingertips and pressed them to your forehead, before returning inside.

■　■　■

I knew in the morning you'd be gone, but I was no longer angry. Mom paced the living room, moving your books, knocking the dust off shelves. I left for the greenhouse without her.

A cool breeze circled the air, and the sprinklers were on in the yard. I knew when I entered. Where you had curled into the grass, now stood a tree. New to the earth. Barely a sapling. Grey trunk. Shades of green. The slender branches stretched up to the sides as if taking a breath after a long nap. This was you.

I could feel your joy. It rose in my chest like a flock of birds. Your leaves danced lightly, and I reached to weave my fingers through them. You are here, you said. I repeated. Our smiles would match. If Mom were there, we would be a complete triangle. Something whole. However, I couldn't imagine it. Her touch and gaze and presence. All intangible. There was only me and you. The way it always was.

I didn't speak to Mom, after. Instead, I let myself wander. Out the side gate. Past my car. Past the other houses. And other trees. Other sisters. Other Moms. The sunrise was a soft yellow. Lemon color. It tasted sweet, not sour. I breathed it all in.

A LETTER TO MY UNBORN SON

Devin Porter

A LETTER TO MY UNBORN SON

Devin Porter

To My Unborn Son,

The greatest day of my life is going to be when you're born. It's gonna be better than those BBQs at my grandpa's house with the mac cheese, collard greens, and the unlimited supply of Lil' Hugs. It's gon' be better than the day, I officially became Mr. "Bachelor Degree."

When my little prince is born, I get to go by a new name.

Dad.

I could see us now. On a beautiful summer day, we kickin' it poolside. You gonna be sitting there with your Tropical Blast Capri Sun & me with my Vincent's Vineyard Chardonnay. Sip, Sip. Drank, Drank. We livin' on the edge, baby!

Fatherhood ain't no joke, though. The thoughts actually of being one, one day, speed through my mind 24/7 like rush hour traffic on the New York City subway. I wonder how your mind works. "Dad, why aren't there anymore dinosaurs? Dad, why can't I see my eyes? Dad, does the moon taste like a quesadilla? Dad, Dad, Dad, Dad, Dad! No matter what they ask, Daddy should have all the answers.

When I see that smooth, flawless, and innocent skin, I don't want one tear coming down my baby's face. As your father, I promise that nothing in the world would ever hurt you. I am your guardian angel. I am your rock. I am your protector. The dangerous myth of the missing black father ain't got shit on me. Daddy always got you. No matter how old you get.

One. (Beat.) You're learning to walk. Over there stuck doing the permanent little chicken dance.
You wobble and wobble till you fall smack on your face like a domino. You fall again, again, and again, but you always get up. Full of smiles and happiness. Ain't nothing in the world gonna keep you down. You are strong. You are courageous. You are blessed.

Five. (Beat.) You got your sea legs now, but you got that crackhead energy. "Let's play cops and robbers, Dad! You the cop. I'm the robber. Ready, set, go!" Hold on, before we play you need to understand that you shouldn't run from the police. The police protect us from the bad the guys, but sometimes the police interactions don't go as they should. You should never run. "It's just a game, Dad! Try and catch me!"

Ten. (Beat.) "In school today we learned about Rosa Parks. Was Rosa Parks a bad guy? Was that why she was arrested on the bus? Because the police protect us from the bad people, right?" No, Rosa Parks wasn't bad. She's was—she was just—she was just tired. The same way I'm tired of you tryna walk home instead of waiting for me to come pick you up at the bus stop. You follow my rules. You understand me?

Fourteen. (Beat.) Boy, I want you in this house by 7:30. Not 7:31. Not 7:32. I said 7:30. I don't want you outside when the streetlights is off. Cause even though you live on Long Island. Even though you got a white picket fence. Even though if you ain't no criminal. Your daddy ain't no criminal. Your momma ain't no criminal. You even got Max the Maltese. They will look at you different. You're not like the rest of your friends, son.

Sixteen. (Beat.) Trayvon Martin, William Chapman II, Tamir Rice, Michael Brown, Ahmaud Arbery. You are not gonna be like them. Imma keep you safe because that's what I promised to do. That's my job as a father.

Eighteen. (Beat.) Hey now, I know I can be a little overprotective, but you ain't gotta leave me. You can stay here at home with me and your mom. I know you wanna conquer the world, but we can work this out. It's just— it's just—

Sometimes I wish Black Lives actually Mattered.

I wish this war against police brutality wasn't so real because even with all the helicopter parenting in the world, I don't have an answer for this. Hopefully, I get one of the lucky ones.

Sincerely,
Every Black Man in America

ECHOES

Xenia Taiga

ECHOES

Xenia Taiga

One early morning off the coast of Africa, a storm brewed. There, among the rising, warming water and the humid air, it gathered strength, swirling at one hundred and eighty-five miles per hour, collecting the rain and thunder and lighting. The storm swirled toward the Caribbean islands then to us; it came lashing through the eleven states, leaving behind its damages. It was this storm that brought the mermaids.

We noticed them and thought it was our eyes fooling us, but closer looks using our binoculars revealed them to be mermaids. The mermaids found refuge on the cluster of rocks that spread out not far from the beaches. Reaching them was impossible unless you had a boat, but people came nevertheless. Cars and trucks and swarms of bodies crowded our cramped roads, the narrow strips of our beaches, and filled up our small coastal inns' cash machines.

In our town in a certain area, there was a beach's strip where laid several groups of rock islands connecting to each other, and at low tide you could walk out to those islands, but still the raging waters and deep sea prevented us from reaching the largest and farthermost island. Here was where the assembly gathered, here was the best place to view them, here was where the wind whipped the strongest, the waves towered the highest, here you could hear them, the cooing and the growling, the fighting birds soaring on the wind squawking among them, and here was where the first mermaid died.

A man jumped into the deep choppy waters. The waves clashed and pushed against him until he reached the rock the where the mermaids resided. He pulled himself up and climbed the rock's steep ragged formations toward them. The audience on the beach roared as they filmed him. He reached the top and stood. The wind pummeled through his wet his t-shirt and shorts and hair. He held his arms out in victory stance. The mermaids scurried to the edges flapping their tail fins, hissing and snarling. He ran after them, tripping and falling among the rock's many jagged edges. The mermaids pushed themselves off, jumping into the ocean. The crowd on the beach held their binoculars and watched, holding their breath until his hands caught tight the edge of a mermaid's tail. She was a small mermaid, a young one perhaps. She twisted her body and hissed, she flailed her bright pink arms and hands to fight, but he was strong. He quickly pulled her tail over the rocks between his legs and clasped her wrists together, dragging her up and over his shoulders, then he carefully walked toward the edge. The mermaid thrashed. She swung her head violently back and forth, flapped her tail against his back and face, but he was determined, and his hold on her was firm. The gathering on the rock had an inflatable boat with a rope attached to it. They threw it into the sea. The wind pushed the boat around in the air, but the men held onto the rope. Another man then dove into the waters. His hands grabbed the flying boat's outer rim. He climbed into the boat. From the crowd on the rock, an oar appeared and was thrown to him. He caught it, then rowed to the rock where the man and captured mermaid waited. They plopped into the boat. The men on the rock filed into a line and together they tugged on the rope pulling the boat to the rock they stood where they lifted and carried her across the rock islands to the shore. The crowd was ecstatic but calm as they stood in line waiting for their turn to pose with the mermaid. She was passed from arm to arm, hand to hand, camera to camera.

She died two hours later.

All the beaches along the coastline were roped off. Police cars blocked, parked, and cluttered the streets. White vans and black trucks were everywhere. Workers dressed in white lab coats walked to the beach and strolled among the rocks. Yellow *Police Line Do Not Pass* tape linking from benches to cars' bumpers to trash cans shook in the wind. Helicopters flew and dropped nets into the waters and over the rocks. The media camped nearby filming and reported their speculations. In the evening the local sheriff's announcement blasted across the nation's nightly news. He explained they were moving the mermaids to a safe and secure place. He said the mermaids posed a threat to the public's safety. What threats we did not know, but we trusted him. Nobody liked threats this we knew.

Mermaids became a worldwide sensation. They were on everyone's minds. Popstars sang songs about them. Mermaids this, Mermen that. Guitars screeched and howled, drums pounded in dramatic rhythm. Singers sang of love in the sea, fins and scales, their voices howling and echoing. Old blockbusters movies were released in special batches at the IMAX cinemas. *Splash, The Little Mermaid, Pirates on the Caribbean: On Stranger Tides*. The number one popular name for newborn girls was Ariel. For Halloween, everyone's (both young and old, male and female) favorite costume was Ariel's outfit. People who made their living swimming like mermaids were interviewed. Then came the science of it all, and this brought a darker tale that skimmed through our conversations. The scientists blamed the mermaids' miracle on global warming. The oceans were getting too warm, they said. The oceans have been warm for a long while now, they warned. The mermaids came to the rocks for a new life. There the shores' winds helped cool their skins. It was only a matter of time, they said.

Special documentaries aired on TV and they showed us where the mermaids were held. They were held in tanks, in buildings, in small above the ground swimming pools. The scientists explained to us what they had learned from their observations. There are no male mermaids, they announced. Only females. The females reproduced whenever they felt like it. Basically, they were like chickens or Cockatiels or seahorses, they said. And no, they did not have the intellectual capabilities like humans. They were very much like animals. The program showed a glimpse of them. It was a dark grainy video. A water tank inside a building with no widows. Eerie howling pierced the cold damp air. A bucket full of fish was dumped into the tank. Blood filled the tank as large bodies with tails swam and swirled in the waters. Nearing the clip's end, the camera zoomed in on the worker holding a large tuna fish in midair. He stood on a ladder and leaned forward dangling the fish above the pool. The camera caught and froze the moment she leaped out of the waters. Her breasts were bare, her long hair was tangled, her skin wet, her teeth pointy and bloody. That image quieted us, that image played itself over and over, on the television, on the commercials, in our heads at night while we slept and we all silently came to the same conclusions that mermaids were mermaids. They were like fish, they were like chickens, they were like cows, they were not like humans.

But we forgot all about our concerns when Water World down by the sea had mermaids available for public viewing. Families and their young children, old couples, newlyweds, and recently appointed license-holding teenagers drove their cars down to the shores not too far from where the infamous incident had happened many years ago and parked their cars inside Water World's large parking lots paying the outrageous ticket entrance fee.

The mermaids were in the back by the ocean near the dolphins' pens. There were three small above ground pools and here you could see them. Large warning signs translated in five languages were posted by the pools: *Be Careful with Your Hands! They Bite!*

The mermaids in the pools were like adolescents, of medium size, freely swimming around. A few of us, however, leaned over and looking down toward the bottom saw on the mermaids' fins a punctured hole which was connected to a chain that was nailed to the bottom of the pool. Their faces were like humans, but their teeth were long and pointy like snarling German Shepherds. They had varying degrees of personality. Some were aggressive and hungry. They swam at fast speed, circling the pool walls around and around looking for the free fish handouts. Others were shy and stayed toward the middle of the pool at the bottom resting, collecting the torn bits and pieces that floated, stuffing it into their mouths. They came up sometimes breaking the pool's surface with their squeaking but quickly went back to the bottom to hide with the other shy ones. A few were neither. These eagerly looked for interactions with us. They popped up over the pool's walls, leaned their arms over the edges and waited for us to give them fish. These were the ones you had to be careful with; they looked almost human, too human. They too, like the dolphins next to them loved to eat fish, but unlike the dolphins if you came too close, their hands grabbed you, their crazed eyes looked into yours, and their voices squealed a high pitched sound. No one knew what they were saying.

Some people were disturbed. Others weren't. They took selfies.

The bigger mermaids were placed in the large dome exhibit. It was a big tank complete with a kelp garden and water pumps to mimic the ocean's waves. It was a perfect world of stingrays, bat stars, leopard sharks, kelp bass, pacific sardines, California sheepheads, and eels swimming among the rocks and swaying seaweed. The view was hypnotic as the sun shone and the different hues of green and blue shadows flickered between the waving kelp and fish. It reminded us of past carefree summer days spent at the beach and swimming pools. The dark suggested something else all together of secrets and dangers.

If you stood still, deep in the thicket of the kelp, you could catch a glimpse of a baby mermaid. We could never get a good look at their faces. Their lush hair flowed down their backside and spread out into a halo around their faces. They swam fast as if our stares burned them, darting like bullets between the towering kelp forests, disappearing behind the rocks.

The older ones were different, bigger and their hair trailed past their fins. If you pressed your face against the glass, they would come for you. They swam as if they had all the time in the world, they swam as if they had swum forever. They swam frolicking their bodies in the waters' waves, caressing the vibrations. They swam as if they were teasing us, as if we were lacking something in our human bodies, as if they were perfect and we were imperfect.

We noticed the scars. The thick and thin scars that marked their hands, backs, stomachs, and faces. Where did these come from? Did they come from their time spent fighting in the oceans, fighting for survival among each other and other large sea creatures or were they inflicted by us? We didn't know and there was no way to ask them.

The mermaids we saw in the beginning on the documentaries were limpid, vicious and evil, their skin pink and raw as if they suffered a bad sunburn, but under Water World's regulated water cooling temperatures and the healthy abundance of foods, their health improved. Their skin shone. They became white like ghosts or spirits. They were revived, alive like the mermaids of before, of the stories and legends that we have heard, and it was at this time that the howling began.

Their howling lasted up to a full ten minutes or longer, consisting a wide variety of whistles, clicks, squeals, and groaning. It was assumed this was their way of exerting their verbal communication skills, like the whale songs in the deep oceans; whatever the reasons were, they were noisy. In the morning they eeked with the fighting sea gulls. At night they squeaked with the croaking sea lions.

They screamed so much the dolphins jumped out of their pools, laying out on the pavements gaping and flapping, turning into desperate creatures in need of help. The animals were separated and relocated to other areas of the park. Where exactly they were moved to, we did not know, and in the tank it became harder and harder to spot them. Even if we came early in the morning before the crowds, we still couldn't find them and all the pounding in the world did not bring them out of the kelp forest. Hearing our displeasure, a knowing person would step up between us and tell us, "There are no mermaids. Used to be, sure. But not anymore." That was when we saw the newly posted sign next to the tank: PLEASE DON'T POUND THE GLASS. In smaller print it warned us: *Sometimes you will not see the mermaids. Brooding mermaids are easily frightened and quickly irritated which can have a detriment effect on their young ones. Please be respectful.*

We read this. We understood this. But we got bored with facts.

We got bored looking at the kelp and fish circling the tank. We touched stingray fish before. We kayaked through thick kelp before. We snorkeled off islands and dove through swarms of tropical fish and sea creatures where later we danced the night away drinking the localized specially made coconut flavored cocktails. Those experiences were much better than staring at this exhibit of nothing. Our stomachs growled for us to nibble something, and we left thinking about the mermaids. Perhaps they were moved again. To a better place. A bigger place. One with no windows. In a tank built for war. As we waited at the drive-thru for our ice coffees and french fries, we realized they were probably dead. We imagined the workers' reaction finding the lifeless mermaids floating in their small pools. We liked to think their bodies were lifted out to the ocean and at sun set given a fitting burial, but instead, probably, they were chopped up and mashed into puppy chow, because nobody liked to waste now days.

Via Internet we discovered the mermaids were on display in other places. They left California in specialized box-crate bathtubs, riding inside semi-trailer trucks to Texas and Florida. Then soon they were everywhere. Tokyo, Beijing, Africa, Belgium. Everyone, either on television or in person, had seen one. We all had a key chain, photographs, or a postcard up on our refrigerators. The popular mermaid songs' lyrics played on repeat in our heads. People tired of hearing their howling, became bored with their hiding, and they, like us, stopped coming as well. And truth be told, those lyrics weren't all that great.

Water World adapted to the new changes. In the mermaids' former spots, they set up rollercoasters. New blockbuster movies were released containing no mermaids. We moved on to other things. Bigger things. Things bigger than mermaids. We waited for E.T.

E.T. never came. After several years people started to ask about the mermaids. Where were they exactly? Were they okay? Were they kept in science labs? Were they experimented on? What was the story with the scars on their bodies? Why were they howling? People with big hearts filled up their gas tanks and drove down to the beaches and to Water World's parking lots to hold their homemade signs. They demanded answers. PETA urged us to write letters to the president. The protesters managed to temporarily halt the few showings that existed, but the police came, and they left because their permits had expired.

In hindsight it seemed like they were always howling, we just didn't pay attention. Besides, the roller coasters drowned out their eekings. And Water World did something, we didn't know exactly what, but something. It was quiet. Too quiet.

Some of us had seen what happened. We read their postings of white vans pulling up in the middle of the night into Water World's lots. They had rambling theories of evil scientists and the collaborating government officials. Rumors spread of how most of the mermaids were killed and used as a source for food, which was ridiculous, but still the rumors grew. They were housed in underground government's experimental compounds. They were subjected to cloning. They were in the CIA program and underwent rigorous training. They were clipped with GPS tracking devices and dropped off in the coldest arctic region to regulate global warming, many of them dying in the process. But this was a necessary death. A death to protect humanity. Josh, the janitor drunk, told the story he was''t supposed to tell. "Everybody sold them off," he said. Only a few like Water World kept several on hand in case the public became interested in them again. The mermaids in their possession were sterilized. "They can't have babies," he said and the bar became silent for a moment. "Two's enough. If they want babies, they said the scientists have them stocked somewhere."

"Where?" we asked.

"In places like in Nevada. Places we're not supposed to know about. But we can get two more, if we want. They have a contract. It's a written contract. I've seen it. We can get as many as we want. You just need to know who to talk to."

Josh was fired. He had three kids and a sick wife with an unknown illness. He went door to door asking for leftovers, most of us pretended we weren't home.

One evening the whole town echoed with their shrieking, it lasted for two hours, setting off a chain reaction with the neighborhood dogs. In the morning we learned some young ones had too much to drink. They decided to invade Water World. Mermaids' body parts and hair strands were scattered throughout the parking lot.

The things that were going on. It didn't feel right. Even Sheriff Tom agreed, but what could you do? The place gave them jobs. Remember when Water World looked for new construction workers? Remember when our towns and inns and restaurants and grocery stores were filled with tourists and cash came pouring in? Who could complain? It was really only the fishermen who griped, and they had been grumbling long before the mermaids came. It wasn't till the mermaids came into the spotlight did the fishermen remember their complaints, and now their resentments and bitterness had been stirred up again, since they now had someone they could point their fingers at, someone to blame.

"The damn government saying we can't fish," they said. "Saying we need to let the oceans rest. Saying it's our fault. It wasn't us, it never was! It was those damn mermaids! They were the ones eating up all the fish. We just didn't know until now." They slug down their beers and cursed the mermaids over and over. "Those damn mermaids," they said. They shook their heads and asked for another drink.

The mermaids were like dogs in how they would often howl in warnings. They were like dogs in alerting everyone that the postman was arriving or in predicting a great earthquake was about to occur. They were like dogs, but the dogs were nicer.

Deep in the night they'd rouse us from our sleep, and so many mornings afterward we'd wake up to find the debris dispersed in our town, the twisted trees' roots exposed to the air, our roof shingles scattered over our front lawns and down the streets, parking lots and basements flooded and as we carefully walked around the broken glass and fallen wires, we'd mentioned to each other, our voices full of curiosity, "Didn't we hear the mermaids last night?"

Each storm brought the howling and in our houses we ambled from one room to the next, pressing our faces and palms against the windows panes, trying to gauge if this was the big one, the one that would force us out of our homes, force us out of our land, force us to finally realize we could not live the way we have always lived. We stepped outside our houses to look at the sky, to feel the air pressure. We went back inside and turned on the radio to hear the latest weather reports. During commercials we doubted our ears and thought maybe the strange eeking was perhaps a cat's soulful meowing or a whimpering dog hiding underneath our porches, but we could never find the dog or cat, and standing again on the porch we looked up at the sky, studying it, trying to find the answers we needed and there underneath our feet we felt the wind rattling the porches' boards loose. The gusts played with our windowpanes and shutters, bent the porch swing, and twisted our pink flamingo lawn ornaments. Waves sloshed over the seawalls with a majestic force. The mermaids' sirens grew boisterous and deafening. We went back in our houses, pulling our prepacked backpacks from our closets. We jiggled the car keys in our hands wondering, whether or not we should leave, when the mermaids' song again drifted with the winds.

We stood still and listened. What were they trying to tell us? It was a melancholy sound. A voice full of mourning and sadness. A sound that broke your heart, but there was something else, too. There was bitterness and spite. And this made our hearts skip a beat, for this could only mean that something big was going to happen, that whatever it was, it was destined to be bigger than the last one, bigger than the one that brought the mermaids. It was going to be big. It was going to tear us off the face of this earth.

The rain came down hard, the waves thrashed, windows broke, our cars alarms blared and the mermaids' chorus became louder than before. Goose bumps traveled up our arms, the hair on our arms and the back of our necks prickled with fear as the waters rose over our feet. Rushing down the steps to our cars, the waters now came to our knees and we feared it may be too late when we heard the mermaids again. Their songs reminded us and we saw them; their tail fins slashing about in the water tanks, their hands clawing at the tempered glass walls, their voices, collectively, higher and shriller, as their words stung our ears: *you deserve this you deserve this you deserve this.* We stood there our knees shaking, our hearts sinking, our arms turning numb, our ears ringing as we realized they were not warning us; they never were.

SEVERAL WAYS TO REMOVE YOURSELF

Erin Piasecki

SEVERAL WAYS TO REMOVE YOURSELF

Erin Piasecki

One option is oil. Slick and murky and viscous. You make yourself glossy. Coconut or olive or grapeseed. Stay away from motor. Nothing crude. Sweep along ankle into thigh. Grease the shin bone thoroughly. Pop a finger into your mouth to coat the inside. You walk a slippery path to the bathroom, your knees buckling. Find yourself waiting in the mirror, coated in a thin sheen of piss-yellow. It didn't work; it often doesn't. Still, you must start somewhere.

Maybe it started with your mother. Her comments about her smattered freckles, her skin, prodding along her hairline and plucking out strays. A rancid, sticky dissatisfaction with her body.

The next method takes longer. You shrink. Become smaller than the space. Over the next few months you make your transformation. Whittle apples with surgical diligence. Pop each shard one by one into parted lips. Because you are committed to this removal, you eventually refuse anything at all. Drink only sips of tea in even numbers. Busy your hands by peeling the rinds off fruit. You pick things that are more labor than reward. Oranges. Furry kiwis. Arrange their skins in tidy piles, but do not touch their meat. Eating flesh means you remain flesh.

Skin has always bothered you. You are allergic to parabens, to imidazolidinyl urea, to phenoxyethanol. You used to scrape your nails across the rind of you; pull up brown zest from underneath your fingernails. Your mother would jab beneath your nails with a sharp instrument, then wipe the gunk onto paper towels. After, the instrument would soak in a small Tupperware of blue disinfectant.

You search the internet, face blued by the phone screen. Photos of cakes made to look like inanimate objects. An array of skincare products arranged painstakingly across a lavender bedspread. You read a post about a man who made a doll out of his lover when she died. Painted her face and dressed her. Romantic, the commenter prods.

In the mirror, you come to terms with your state of being here / in body / in place. Look at yourself. The cut of thigh just between two splotches of toothpaste. You turn away, try to forget what you've seen. The world around you is not so awful. True, your apartment is a dark eye socket. But press the tip of your nose into something that smells good. There is a clutch of tulip bulbs in the corner. Inside a crystal vase from your mother. No, those are dead. Nevermind.

Taste something decadent. Scoop expensive facial cream into your mouth. Dip hands into honey, organic lubricant. Splash glitters across cheekbones, temples, into your hairline. They stick to the honey. In the mirror, you expect to glint back. Instead, you are flat, tacky, covered in grease and trash that will cling to the sink for months. To the sink, to the floor, to the cabinets, to your teeth. Pull a sparkle from between your gums. Wipe your finger against a square of toilet paper. Glitter, blood.

All your beauty products are a cityscape on the bathroom counter. All these things your mother sent you as non-apologies. For screaming at you on the phone you got a subscription to a skincare curation box, an apple face foam; for jabbing her nails into your arms, a facial mask made from pepperberries that stains your skin artificial, bright purple.

These things do not matter. Prod your eyelids apart. Make yourself see. Not just look but see. Maybe one day you will get out of this room. Stop daring yourself to assess the cuts of flesh and juice and skin. Jamming your finger into soft bruisy spots like picking fruit at the supermarket.

Crawl beneath your bed. Try to shut out all light.

She wanted you to remain young as a green banana. When you were young, you were Sweet and Precocious and Gangly and Lean.

Remember your mother lathering you with lotion, cream, balm. Mother slicing tags off shirts. Mother spraying you with clobetasol, which made your breath smell like fruit. Remember your sensitive skin, always pink and exposed in a flaky white pith. Blotches like hickeys across your cheeks. A firework of red.

You were there that day.

No, you weren't.

You cut it from your memory with a paring knife.

Let yourself be eaten / out. Eaten right out of your pajama shorts. Eaten right out of your skin. You enjoy the idea more than the actual performance. The knobby bent knees of it. The shaved pussy of it. The hairy pussy of it. The entire pink shuffle, the salty cum, the moments after.

He says, You didn't seem to like it, and you know he means It and Him and Your Own Body and all Bodies, any

Body at all. It seems to you a miracle that anyone could enjoy a body. Its caverns. A sharp lung. Meat wrinkles your nose; all those swirling fat deposits.

You remember a video you saw, only a few seconds long. In it, a woman bends over and lifts her pleated skirt, revealing a puckered pink vortex of anus. At the end, she sticks a coy finger deep inside. You went into her user history and found posts daily. Every day a video. Bend. Skirt. Finger. You wonder now if it changes, depending on the weather. Growing tighter, pursed. A very special type of weather forecaster. Tornadoes hitting the valley and the anus sucking the woman in.

To recover from this image, you take four edibles and lie on the floor quivering. Melting into shitty shag carpet. Let every breath press your abdomen further into the ground, into the earth, down to the molten core, back up to the belt digging against your belly button. Decide to redo your life. Maybe you will become a different person. You think of the food in your fridge. Mayonnaise in a giant jar. Spooning your hand inside. Your stomach, the belly button again, that woman's asshole. The plasticity of it.

You try the oil method once more, but this time substitute mayonnaise. Try to slip out from inside yourself.

Back to the post online, the man and his doll-lover: Actually, the man was her stalker. She didn't want him. He did something like paper mâché over her dead face. He put a cardboard tube like one in the middle of paper towels inside her. A fake cunt.

Yes, it was your mother. Her fault, her fault, her fault. Mother in her casket, mother painted like a cake, mother belly-up, mother pickled by formaldehyde, mother who will rot, mother already beginning to.

When the mayonnaise does not work, you submerge yourself in scalding liquid. Cut a small X across scalp, both soles of the feet, below the peasant ankles. Fish yourself out with a slotted spoon and into a prepared ice bath. Peel back the skin with a knife or fingers. It slips off like a charm. You let the skin crinkle and fold in on itself. There is a little pit inside but ignore that. Focus.

How smooth the fruit underneath. How ripe.

THE SHOE
WHICH KNEW
IT WAS A
LOAF OF
BREAD

Lucy Duggan

THE SHOE WHICH KNEW IT WAS A LOAF OF BREAD

Lucy Duggan

No matter how hard it tried, the shoe could not convince anyone that it was a loaf of bread.

It was a handmade artisan shoe, made to fit the foot of a man who did not walk much anymore.

It had known for a long time, or perhaps it had always known, that it was actually a loaf of handmade artisan bread. Every time the man put his left foot into the shoe, it was an insult and an injury.

It is hard to know whether the right shoe also suffered from this problem of misinterpretation. The two shoes had never discussed it.

Since the man did not walk much anymore, the shoes were left in the corner of the Utility Room. Despite its name, most of the objects in the room were broken or too old-fashioned to be of any use.

It is generally assumed that two shoes prefer to be stored side by side as a pair, but as far as we know, nobody has ever asked any shoes their opinion on this.

The shoe which knew it was a loaf of bread no longer had a shoelace threaded through the ten holes in its crust. Perhaps an ordinary shoe would have felt bereft. The lace had broken when the man's sister had only been trying to help! She had pulled the broken pieces out of the holes and thrown them into a corner of the Utility Room.

The right shoe still had its lace, although it was slightly frayed.

The mice who lived in two nests in the Utility Room did not consider the shoe to be a loaf of bread. That is, they did not gnaw on it or chew its crust, and nor were they tempted by its smell. The mice from the first nest, behind the broken washing machine, preferred to wolf down crumbs of toast which were left in the kitchen where the man ate his breakfast. The toast was made from spongy blocks of white bread from the supermarket. The shoe which knew it was a loaf of bread was quite well aware of that and considered it an irony.

The mice from the second nest, behind the damaged painting, devoted a high proportion of their time to nibbling on a stained sofa cushion and pulling out the fluffy white stuffing. The stuffing was presumably not good to eat; perhaps they used it to line their beds. In the past, they had feasted on sugar which was spilt on the table after the man drank his tea. Now, the man took sweeteners in his tea. The sweeteners could not so easily be spilt and did not appeal to the mice. So the mice looked for crumbs of ginger biscuits and slivers of cheese, though the man no longer ate much of either of those things.

(In the past, the shoe which knew it was a loaf of bread had given a lot of thought to the man's eating habits. But at some point, this began to seem futile.)

It can be assumed that the man's cat took the same view as the mice: that the shoe was not a loaf of bread. She always stalked past both shoes without paying any attention to either of them. When the man's sister threw the broken shoelace into the corner of the Utility Room, the cat pounced on the longer piece of shoelace and bit it, rolling on her back and attacking it as if it were a snake.

That, for the shoe, was a rare moment of gratification.

The man's sister made an exasperated sound, like a sole scuffing hard on the ground.

She had put her back out when she tried to help the man with his shoes.

And then he had not even wanted to go out for a walk.

She might be younger than him, but she was not as young as she used to be, she said, even though nobody was listening to her, because the man had shuffled back to the sitting room in his slippers. He had turned the radio on very loud and the announcer said, a pair of shoes worn by Elvis Presley, but the man switched to a channel playing ear-splitting guitar sounds and cut off the end of the story.

No one was getting any younger, the man's sister murmured, looking at the damaged painting.

The shoe did not agree. It could feel itself growing fresher and fresher, and it knew for certain that one day it would become a lump of raw, sticky dough, bubbling with yeast that was undeniably alive.

MAGICALLY DELICIOUS

Pearl A. Griffin

MAGICALLY DELICIOUS

Pearl A. Griffin

Monday...

Cereal. I can't stop eating it. Doesn't even matter what kind—it's all fucking awesome. Other than keeping this new human alive, it's the most important thing in my life now. My baby's name is Lauren. She looks a bit like Kermit the Frog, the Muppet Baby version. Her eyes bug out, and her mouth is always open a little. She's wrapped tightly, all swaddled up in this baby pillow thing my aunt gave me. Well not an aunt, exactly—Tia was my mom's best friend when I was little. She watched me when mom went on days-long binges and then took me in for a bit when I was fifteen, tried to get me through high school as best she could.

I didn't hate being pregnant. It was like growing a little bestie. And even after I knew I'd be doing this alone, it seemed okay. We could do our own thing, me and this baby. Nobody to tell us not to eat cereal all at once in the middle of the night.

"Only sometimes," I'd say, rubbing my watermelon belly.

But it's not sometimes. I think it's all I've eaten since I left the hospital yesterday. Or today? I haven't slept yet, so maybe that counts as still today, even though it's three a.m. tomorrow. Apparently giving birth is fucking traumatic. Original, I know. But seriously? It felt like a horror movie murder. I swear that baby was half the size of me as she pushed her way out. Being born can't be a picnic, either. Talk about a hard first day. It's a good thing we don't remember that shitshow. Just think—safe, warm, protected by another mammal's survival instinct, then bam! Life.

You've probably heard that breakfast is the most important meal of the day. But the thing about cereal is that you can eat it whenever. Like right now. I just shoved a huge ass bite of Fruit Loops in my trap. And holy fuck, it's good! You know that feeling from when you were a kid and someone hugged you after a long, hard day of just being a kid and you felt, for a minute, that you were safe? This is just like that. Except I'm about to also feel fat, which is of course what being a grown up is all about.

Lauren is heavy in my arms. God, she's huge! If I don't prop one of my elbows up on a pillow, my arm will literally fall off. At the hospital they taught me how to get her latched—weird thing to say about my own body, right? Latched. Anyway, seemed like she ate gallons. But now we're here—the nurses kept saying "home," but that's not the right word for it—and she will only guzzle for a minute or two at a time before she stops and stares at me with those globe eyes of hers.

Me and Lauren are living in this tiny room. We have a couch that turns into a bed, but it's always a bed and fills up most of the space. Better than a mattress on the floor. A neighbor downstairs found this couch out on the street for free. Nothing wrong with it. He helped me carry it in, and I vacuumed it real good and Febrezed it a few times to fight the stale cigarette smell. As long as I keep the window cracked, I don't even notice it anymore.

I rest the bowl of Fruit Loops on Lauren's belly and try not to let the milk dribble down my chin. I ate cereal every day when I was a kid. It was the only type of breakfast I really even knew about until I saw that scene in *All Dogs Go to Heaven* when the little girl is eating waffles with her new family. Maybe I knew about waffles before that, but that's when I remember wanting them instead of cereal. Or maybe I just wanted someone to make them for me.

When I was a kid, my mom only ever bought the knock-off cereal brands. You know, the ones in the bags that taste like chalk versions of the good stuff.

"It's the same thing!" she exasperated over the nails-on-a-chalkboard sound of my whining.

"It is NOT!" I pitched, high as I could before mom's temples throbbed visibly and she grabbed me by my hair. Her face got real close to mine so I could see the veiny red lines reaching towards her pupils.

"Knock it off," she said. Even then I knew better than to say "or what."

Definitely Tuesday

It's only been two days, but the only TV is in mom's room. This makes two days seem like the last part of the school year: forever-taking. I would have graduated a year ago if I'd stuck with it. I know a few who did, but they don't have jobs either and have to live with their parents too. I wouldn't say I dropped out so much as stopped going. That's why I had to leave aunt Tia's the first time. Her only rule was stay in school. I know a few girls who quit school because they got pregnant, but I'm the only one who got pregnant because I quit school. What else do you do with that much time on your hands? Guess Tia had a point about staying busy.

Lauren fills up space like a baby should—still she seems smaller now than she did before. I lean to the right and to the left, inspecting her naked body on the changing mat. I swear there was more to her when I brought her here. There's a tug down behind my belly button that makes me feel almost sick, like I need to bend over and hold my middle to keep my guts from falling out. This is what parenting feels like.

I reach down into the box of Honey Nut Cheerios I wedged between the arm of the couch and the wall. I can clench a handful from where I'm sitting, but soon I'll have to scoot over closer in order to reach. The sound of my teeth crunching down on the cereal is loud in my ears, but not nearly as loud as the wail Lauren lets out as I re-diaper her.

"Trust me, kid. I get it," I say. The hospital sent me away with these giant-ass pads, which I've learned are basically diapers for my horror show vaginal recovery. I don't know what's worse, the stabbing pain in my back or the constant moist feeling.

"Shh, shh, shh," I say, but it sounds weird between us. Girls should never be shushed. "How
'bout a story?"

"There once was a girl," I begin. It's hard to remember any stories, but then again maybe I never knew any.

"There once was a girl who had an evil mother, or step-mother, or maybe there was a witch..."

Lauren screams louder, and I hear stomping from my own mother's room next to ours, and then drawers banging. It's as if she needs to remind us she's there and can hear the crying and that noise drives her to drink. Scooping my baby up close to my neck, I breathe deep, and soon Lauren breathes with me like we're a pair of lungs. The banging stops, and I lay her in the nook of my crossed legs. Her diaper slides wonky on her hips like it's too big. Can't be though—babies don't get smaller, do they?

I pull up my shirt, but she doesn't latch right away. She squirms against me, making a little rodent sound. Finally, she gets ahold of me, gurgling like I'm too big for her. I prop her up, which helps a bit. I imagine it tastes like the milk mixture leftover in the bottom of the bowl after the cereal is gone. I gag.

Even as a kid I hated the leftover milk. It seemed old by the time you were done—elderly, gray, old milk. My mom made me drink it when I was little. I cried big tears into the bowl and drank those too. I got a little older and started to refuse.

"It's wasteful," she growled.

"It's gross," I replied.

After a few broken bowls, I learned to add more cereal to the milk until it was almost entirely soaked up. But then, sometimes I'd pour too much cereal and need more milk and the whole thing would start again.

"Alice!" Mom's yell was like a tornado—a funnel of sound and debris heading right for you. She could shake a house and clear the street with that voice. My own was the squeak of a wheel running along an empty street through the rubble.

"Whaaat?" but as soon as I said it, I remembered.

"Did you eat this *whole* bag of cereal?"

Thing is, I did. She knew it. I knew it. But I said "no"

anyway. An entire box of Lucky

Charms was churning in the bottom of my belly.

"Are you fucking kidding me?" My mom hurled the empty bag at me, but it was too light to send the message she was going for, so she threw the empty bowl too. It crashed against my raised forearms. When it hit the floor, thick chunks of ceramic broke away from each other and slid across the grimed-up tile. After that, I stopped eating breakfast at home.

Wednesday

Have you ever noticed how Tony the Tiger gets more built as he gets older? I saw an old advertisement once for Frosted Flakes, and Tony was this cute little thing. Now he's fucking ripped. I think the opposite is happening to Lauren. She's smaller now. Smaller than yesterday. Kind of like those problems in math books where there are two shapes right next to each other, but one is such and such a percent smaller than the other and you have to find the missing side.

Before I moved into this tiny room, I was staying with my old friend, Katie, in her studio apartment. Back in ninth grade I started eating breakfast at Katie's house. We were best friends that year, and her parents bought the good stuff. They had these pop-top sealing containers for them. Usually Cinnamon Toast Crunch is stale after the first day you open it, but not there. I would show up before school and pour myself a bowl, sit at the high counter, leveraging my legs back and forth to spin the stool. I can still taste how good it felt to be in that house.

When my mom found out I was doing it, she lost it. I mean really lost it. She opened every cabinet in the house, pulling everything inside out with both hands, holding the open bags of cereal upside down until they made neat little ant hills on the floor. But even the ants didn't want the off-brands.

Before Katie's studio, I was staying with aunt Tia and her husband for a bit, and before that the father and his mom and little brother. But every place has a "best by" date. Especially this one. I've lived with my mom off and on since I was fifteen. She's never kicked me out, not really, just makes it so leaving is the only good choice.

"You did this to yourself, Alice," she said, when I left the first time.

"Fuck you," I said, trying my hardest to shut the door like I knew where I was going.

The thing I bet you don't know is that self-loathing is hereditary, like diabetes. It's not guaranteed, but under the right conditions, it gets you. I chew until the cereal in my mouth is just soft enough to swallow, then scoop in another bite. The worst thing ever is soggy cereal. Eating it is a race against the decomposing powers of milk. Otherwise it tastes like melted crayons. But when you get that good crunch mixed with sweet cold milk, there's almost nothing like it.

Lauren lets loose a crackling order.

"Okay, okay," I say like a mantra. My own quiet prayer for her and for me.

I heft her onto my shoulder, but she's so light it's jarring. I lift her up and down with both hands like an offering.

"Fuck." A jolt of fear strikes me, lightning from inside out. She likes the movement, though, so I keep raising and lowering her dwindling body. Once it's clear she won't start crying again, I pull a book about pregnancy and infants out from under the side of the couch. I haven't read a book since tenth grade, including this one, but I swipe the dust off the front with my forearm and open it up. The pages smell like the inside of a cheap thrift store—all dry and stale—and based on the number of jean jackets and overalls in these janky pictures, I think it's older than I am. I don't think I'll find anything in here about shrinking babies.

"There once was a girl," I start. Lauren seems to be listening this time, so I go on.

"And the girl was locked in a tower somewhere. Probably in Europe, where there are towers. And this girl wanted to get out of the tower and go adventuring, but obviously the witch-mother-person wanted to keep her prisoner. The witch was lonely and crazy and drunk."

Thursday/Friday

Most women have cravings during pregnancy, but mine didn't come until I was here, back at mom's. Until I was here and awake in the middle of the night even though the baby was sleeping. And I needed a bowl of fucking cereal. It was so strong that I actually considered asking my mom to go and get me some, but I texted around for a favor instead. It's hard to say no to a girl who's just had a baby, but I have a feeling that only lasts so long.

Lauren is asleep again, so I hoist her up a little farther on my shoulder. She feels like a hand on my heart, huggish and warm. It doesn't suck. I think Lauren would be funny and adventurous if she were to grow big. But she's not. I gave her a bath earlier tonight, and I could hold her with only my palm and forearm. It's not that she's skinny, though. She's just getting smaller. I think maybe I should take her to the doctor.

I wrap little Lauren up tightly—she squirms as best she can in her burrito state. I bring the cereal bowl close to my chin and spoon brightly colored dripping bites into my mouth before the crying starts. She likes to watch my face as I eat, her eyes all buggy and moist. Sometimes I think she's jealous, like if she could take my teeth and use them herself, she would. With each bowl I chow down, it's like Lauren needs it too.

My mom sleeps during the day, so for a long time she didn't notice that I stopped eating the cereal she bought. The bags towered on top of each other on the fridge. Marshmallow Matey's on Apple Zings on Dyno Bites. You see, cereal is a staple when you're on food stamps. You buy cereal and milk. Expensive butter and cheap peanut butter. Mac & Cheese and Hamburger Helper. To this day I can't stand Hamburger Helper. It's fucking disgusting. But give me a box of Honey Smacks and I'll fuck you right now. Weird, right?

Me and Lauren fall asleep together. I dream that we are in a meadow and Lauren is regular baby size—like she needs wide open space in order to grow right. I wake with a jolt when I feel Lauren drop to the bottom of the swaddle. Frantic, I unroll the bundle in my lap. She's there, the size of a guinea pig, no longer sleeping.

"Fuck," I sigh. Relief floods me for a second. A reflex.

Lauren wriggles with a creaky ah, ah, ah. I slide her into the crook of my arm, only I have to be more careful because she nearly slips through the space between my elbow and ribs.

A door closes nearby and I know mom is back. She works the swing shift at Walmart on the weekends. The only way she can get a job is by taking what no one else wants. Works for her, though, since she can sleep all day, then stop at a bar after work. When I was trying to get a job, I said I'd never take a swing shift—I was better than that. But it seems that sooner or later we all do what our mothers did.

Lauren lets out a tiny scream.

"Hungry again?" I say. But then my heart sinks down into my stomach as I wonder if she'll be able to latch at her size. Something is really wrong. I position her as best I can and work my nipple around her mouth. She's mawing at it but can't seem to get anything. I squeeze the end of it, thinking maybe I can spray some out.

To keep her calm, I tell her more of our story.

"The girl in the tower with the witch-mother ran away to find a prince to love. He was super hot and told the girl he loved her. But she grew bored and found another one. She dreamed of climbing all the mountains and swimming all the seas."

A few drops fall from me into Lauren's mouth, which seems to satisfy her. At first I'm relieved, but no, there's no relief here. Tears prick at my eyes, my chest twists. I cry and cry and cry because I never meant to do this. I wasn't going to be a mother. I look down at Lauren through blotchy eyes, and for a terrifying second, I feel nothing. Like I hung all my emotions outside on a line to dry, but now it's raining, and I don't want to go out and get them.

"Just you wait," my mom used to say, "till you have your own kids."

She would then list all of the things I'd ever done that bothered her like it was my fucking horoscope.

"Alice," my mom said through sharp grinding teeth. "I swear to god if you keep leaving dirty bowls around this house, I'm gonna throw them out."

"You can't just get rid of all the bowls," I said.

"Well, is it too much to ask for you to use your fucking brain?"

Use your fucking brain. She said it so often, for so long, that it became a part of me—like tree bark growing around a big rusty nail. Now those words belong to my voice instead of hers. But I don't know what to do. I've never been a mom before, and I don't know any good ones. I think of Katie, imagine her in my place with a baby, her mother and father next to her cooing and grabbing at her perfectly normal infant. I chew the inside of my mouth in any place I can get my teeth on. I don't know what to do. I wipe new, quiet tears from my face and raise Lauren to my mouth. I kiss her face, my lips parted. She tastes like new sweat, and a little like Kix—Kid-tested, Mother-approved.

Saturday

I'm almost out of cereal. I have to pull the bag out and shake it gently to dislodge the last few bits from the multi-colored powder. Some of it gets in my bowl, and I growl. I lean in and blow—the fruity powder wafts over Lauren like fairy dust. She fits in my hand now, so I make a cup shape with my palm and scoop her onto my skin.

"Don't pee on me," I demand, though she's so small I might not even notice. She laughs and kicks, her skin on mine melding us together in a new way. "I mean it, though."

I swing her back and forth then bop her up and down. Her laughter is like the squeak of a hamster, but I feel it light me up. Maybe she'll stay this size. I can put her in my pocket and take her to work when I find a job.

"Just you and me," I say.

I stir my milk around the Cap'N Crunch Berries, making sure each one is moistened just enough. For my final bite, I stare down my nose at the spoonful of color. Just then, Lauren, who is fuzzy in my periphery, rolls from my hand, falls to the table with a clunk.

"Oh fuck!" I yell. I pick her up with both hands and hold her close to my face, which is a mistake because her scream is like a dart in the ear. I guess that means she's okay. Although, I suppose "okay" is relative, since she's the size of one of those baby bananas.

There's a sharp pain in the middle of my chest, like all the sugar I've consumed this week has compressed and shot back up. I feel dizzy. Lauren has cried herself out and is heaving and red. I run my finger along her belly and smile as best I can. It seems to comfort her.

"What the girl didn't know," I say, "is that the witch-mother had cast a spell on her to always bring her back to the tower whenever she got too far away or too happy or too sassy. The girl woke up trapped again, but this time with a baby princess she made herself. But the tower was colder and scarier now, and the girl knew her little princess wouldn't make it."

I never told my mom I was pregnant—she could see it, though, by that point.

"Can't say I'm surprised," she said.

I had a few bags and the hand-me-down baby things I'd gathered. It was going to be harder to move around from place to place now that it wasn't just me. I went into labor only a few days later. Mom dropped me off at the hospital on her way to work.

"That baby's better off inside you," she said. "Things

are shit out here."

Those were maybe the truest words she ever said to me. I took them, held them in my own mouth for too long and swallowed them whole. I cried out from the pain in my womb, and I wished harder than anything that I could keep this baby safe.

Lauren is the size of a Wheatie now. She flails her hands and feet in the air. I feel something like instinct pull at the back of my throat. I shake my head, but what else can I do?

So tiny now. I scoop Lauren up in the spoon. Her cry is a Snap, Crackle, Pop when I hold her up near my ear. I bring her gently down close to my lips and whisper, afraid my voice will split her open.

"In the end, the girl escapes with her princess baby to the meadow—it's wide and bright and shining. And they're the safest they've ever fucking been."

I open my mouth, only a little so that it's more cocoon than cavern, and slide the spoon inside. It's quiet now. I swallow. The pain in my chest is gone, my cravings too. I close my eyes and lean back. I breathe for both of us.

THE BOY WITH THE GLASS ARM

Trista Hurley-Waxali

THE BOY WITH THE GLASS ARM

Trista Hurley-Waxali

No one knows how the boy's arm changed to glass. Hints of the change came out when he started planning trips to the movies during the matinee and only participated in low contact sports. At first his parents thought he wasn't interested in being a jock but then wondered what he did after he cancelled plans to a rock concert. Around this time the teachers learned that the boy was consumed by the idea of protection. As other students claimed the boy said his fragility was a physical part of the body. It was as if one day he had tissue and then the next silica, the element replacing the blood in his left arm and hardened after an intense heat. When the new limb became apparent in the home, his mother praised the boy's caution spirit. What she didn't know was how this fixation was going to fester beyond the actions of a typical teen boy.

The idea appeared after a two-week camping trip deep in an Ontario forest. When he got back, the boy mentioned his arm getting stiff. The parents figured he had a scare since the camp never mentioned any injury. The family doctor examined the arm, and everything came back normal. He was offered physical therapy as maybe the nerves were not registering in certain areas, the regions the boy believed to be glass. But the boy responded well in the monitor and advised if he moved the arm it could shatter. The doctor advised the parents to try and trick the boy into using his left arm, but the boy maintained his truth. Even went as far as doing driving lessons with only his right arm.

"At least he's not drinking and partying like other boys. Plus, this quirk he can grow out of without detox." His mother began praising the boy's obsession as other parents wondered if he should be spending time with their teens. For other than the glass arm, his reputation was that of being quiet and intelligent, almost to where it was impossible to imagine him coming up with such a strong condition and maintaining an illusion. The boy was never the type to call attention to something that could easily come undone.

Naturally when something was different, the bullies would be the first to tease. Then the students who were on that summer trip. To them, seeing the boy leaving his perfectly healthy arm in a sling made them sick. The camp leaders would mock his effort to protect the arm, jerking closer to him in the hallway and watching him squirm. For the boy never wanted to blame anyone for his arm shattering and moved out of their way. The boy felt it was up to him to protect himself since no one else could see the glass. Soon the boy started to avoid crowded hallways and tucked himself away between the library stacks. Eventually the bullies stopped seeking him out and he'd stop avoiding their path. Whereby the two never talked but found a comfortable distance apart.

The boy never felt the sling was enough protection, but it kept his arm close to his chest. Sometimes he would wrap a towel and then keep the fabric together with tensor bandages. The boy also bought a couple travel pillows to rest his elbow while he ate or played board games. His mother liked the boy's effort to be responsible for his own slings, each stained with sweat from an effort not to break. Whereas his father was deeply concerned about the boy's hygiene to meet girls at school since the boy asked them to build a larger shower in the basement. The father felt building it would play into the illusion and reminded the boy that a new shower was not an expense their family was ready to pay.

Even as his father feared the boy's declining relationships with girls, the boy wasn't in the slightest. For he worked hard to foster a friendship with a girl named Cara from the homeroom. If he had a presentation, she would help tie his sling in a fancy bow or make a new one from the fabric stores clearance bin. He tried to lay his arm flat to show her the hardest places, but his muscles would get tense and he'd stop. He felt comfortable with her leaving his left arm between them as they walked, as he trusted she wouldn't break the glass. Cara also went to the mall with him to find hoodies with large enough pockets. She would find ones on the rack that had adequate security and an oversized hood to match.

When it came time for the first parent-teacher meeting, there were general concerns from the boy's parents. They wanted to know if he was still participating with his right hand or even showed interest in using his left. The teacher assured him he was still participating and when it came time to use his left arm, he would ask Cara to assist. The teacher knew there were no medical concerns and still never questioned his behavior, for the only behavior the teachers ever questioned happened later that year.

The boy's homeroom class was in the science lab when the first shot was fired. The echo reverberated off the lockers and the hallway became a wave of screaming voices. Inside the boy's room, the students moved without reason and were shoving their desks to run. The teacher stood up and asked everyone to turn off their Bunsen burners and crouch down under their desk. The boy gripped his left arm as he felt each step of the shooter in the hallway. He scratched his arm until it bled onto the tiled floor; he watched the blood to know he was still alive.

The boy used his right arm to grab his hoodie from the back of his chair. Outside the door, the gunman fired into the steel lock. Parts of the door poured into the room as the teacher began shoving students out of the gunman's way. Amongst the fear, Cara had slipped and hit her head. The gunman watched as she slowly came into a seated position, she blinked to focus as he rested the gun along his left leg. He lifted the barrel and placed the gun inches apart from her skin, she feared as she felt heat. In this moment, time was thick like sand as the boy removed his left arm from his sling and ran over to Cara.

The gunman fired
once into the left shoulder,

once into the abdomen.

Cara was covered in fragments of the boy, protected as the gunman then took his own life. The news reported that the boy's shoulder shattered causing him to bleed out, nothing this boy never learned to fear.

AT THE AIRPORT

Kelly Hill

AT THE AIRPORT

Kelly Hill

Whose fault it is they are in Phoenix instead of Cancun
No one has said it, but Ada fears the blame clearly lies with her since the trip is an early birthday present in honor of her fortieth birthday next month.

According to Ada's husband Kevin, United Airlines is to blame since their original flight to Mexico was cancelled. The new flight time to Cancun is listed in red and lacks believability. Kevin has spoken with three different United Airline employees and all have provided different answers for what time the next flight leaves Phoenix and why the family's suitcases are on a plane bound for Kolkata. Kevin has been too frustrated to properly fuss at his daughters and wife for checking bags in the first place, *Pack light, fly right* an unofficial motto.

As a single person, Ada thoroughly enjoyed air travel. As a single person, she never experienced the headaches most people associate with airports. She recalls that her flights arrived and took off on time and that her luggage always landed with her.

As a married stepmother, the new normal is lost luggage, cancelled flights, a flight where the oxygen masks dropped from above, another where a small fire broke out in the cockpit. The first flight she and Kevin took involved an emergency landing and a frantic call for a doctor. *He's a doctor!* she said, gesturing to Kevin. But since he was a dermatologist, this was not much help to the poor woman suffering a stroke.

Am I mis-remembering how easy it used it be to travel? she recently asked her mother.

You once said that travel was what made life worth living, her mom said.

On whether or not the TSA agent was flirting with Ada when he spent an extra long time studying her license

Ada: I think he was just a weird guy. Unprofessional for sure.

Kevin: He certainly put me in an awkward position. At what point do you call over someone's supervisor?

Natalie: If an ass gets grabbed.

Kevin: At that point I might have laid hands on the guy.

Ada: No one's ass was grabbed.

Natalie: (holds hand out in front of her, as if studying a driver's license) Ada Elise Ellison. Five nine, blue eyes, organ donor. (looks up and gives an exaggerated wink) It's hard not to commit *those* stats to memory.

Ada: For the record, there was no wink.

Olivia: Remember that time our waiter asked Ada for her phone number because he thought she was your daughter?

Kevin: That never happened!

Olivia: He had a man-bun, you called him Bun Man.

Ada: I forgot about that guy. How did I forget that?

The contents of Ada's suitcase

One crochet cover-up, five sundresses, all the shorts and sandals and tank tops in her closet, two bottles of SPF 45 sunscreen, one bottle of aloe vera, back issues of *People*, *InStyle*, and *US Weekly*, one bathing suit she worries she is too old to wear, two bathing suits she is confident she can wear at least one more year, two swim skirts she can't believe she owns, a bag of peanut M&Ms she doesn't plan on sharing, an unopened bottle of lube, a travel size toothpaste and toothbrush, hairdryer, phone charger, a pair of jeans, and a travel size container of her shampoo, which costs quite a bit more than Kevin has been led to believe. He probably wouldn't care the shampoo is so expensive. Sometimes you have no control over the baggage you bring from previous relationships.

The stepdaughters

They are fifteen, leggy, brown-eyed, sharp nosed. Natalie's hair is short and curly, Olivia's longer and curlier. In photographs they have the cultivated air of disgraced royalty. As the nicer twin, Olivia, has never said the following to Ada: *You look pregnant in that shirt, Good luck enforcing that rule, As if I care what you think.*

The girls call Kevin *Dad* when they are happy with him, *Daddy* when they want something, *The Father Figure* when bitching about him. Ada is *A* when they are happy with her, *A-daaaa* when they are not, *Mama A* when they want something. This is fine with Ada, and disappointing to Kevin, who had been hoping for Mama A all the time.

Natalie

Natalie has cycled through the various stages of grief at the prospect of being unable to text her boyfriend Rex while vacationing in Mexico, mostly wallowing in denial, anger, and depression. Do you honestly expect me to not text for a whole week? E-mail instead of texting? (Hysterical laughter followed by hysterical tears). You can't be serious. #Ohmygodyoureserious. #Mylifeisover. #Ihateyouboth.

There are times Ada has more patience for the drama of teen girls than Kevin does. How intoxicating and all-consuming love and life and all its calamitous possibilities are at that age. That she remembers quite clearly.

She also remembers her family vacation, age fifteen, to her grandmother's funeral in Indiana. Other times, her patience is as thin as the crochet cover-up in her suitcase.

A conversation between Ada and Kevin on their first date

Kevin: You were married before?

Ada: Yes. ~~A long time ago, a lifetime ago, it's almost like it happened to someone else it was so long ago. And I don't want to talk about it with you because I already know the face you'll make, and I already know the things you'll say, and I don't want you to look at me that way and say those things to me anymore than I want to have conversations with my ex-husband in my head, but it still happens. We don't argue anymore, and I don't try to seduce him either. Mostly he listens, occasionally he offers practical advice. If I thought I was never going to see you again, or if I thought I could contain the story of my ex-husband into something compact and sturdy, I would tell you *The Story*~~

~~of My First Marriage.~~ This wine is really good. More?

Kevin: I'm still working on my first glass. ~~I wonder if she cheated on him.~~ How long were you married?

Ada: Less than a year. ~~He left me.~~ Have you seen the waiter? I hope he hasn't been swallowed up by the kitchen.

Kevin: ~~I bet she cheated on him.~~ Actually, I'll take that second glass.

Similarities between Ada and Kevin's first wife Cammie

Brunettes

Aversion to the mouthfeel of foods like cottage cheese and flan

Bafflement about why Kevin does the following

  (a) stuffs his socks into a drawer without pairing them up first

  (b) replaces his toothbrush every two weeks

  (c) leaves half-drunk travel mugs of coffee in his car

Frustration / anger that Kevin didn't grasp that saying "Valentine's Day is a ridiculous holiday, and I can't believe people celebrate it" does not mean it is okay to arrive home, empty-handed, on February 14

Silliness after two cocktails, although the silliness looks(ed) very different

Olivia's dream

"Ada was cleaning out her closet, and she kept giving me all these clothes she didn't want. I didn't want them either. The only thing I wanted was this white leather jacket at the back of her closet, and she kept saying she'd already promised it to someone else, but she wouldn't say who."

"Fascinating," Natalie says without looking up from her phone where she has been furiously texting. "Oh wait, I'm lying because no one cares about your dreams. No one cares about anyone else's dream, ever, because dreams are only interesting to the person who has them and that-is-a-fact."

"I wish you had a white leather jacket," Olivia says to Ada. Olivia is so adept at ignoring her twin there are times Ada and Kevin worry about her. "I would borrow that All. The. Time."

"Ada would *never* let you borrow her white leather jacket."

"Nat's right," Ada says. "I wouldn't let that jacket out of my sight."

What other people in Terminal 2 Gate A7 are doing
Reading
Texting
Pretending to read the newspaper while staring at the stepdaughters' legs
Eating
Knitting socks: "I asked for alpaca wool, and he bought cashmere. He said he thought cashmere was better, but I told him alpaca. I even spelled it for him, A-L-P-A-C-A. Don't tell me he didn't hear the word alpaca coming out of my mouth because I won't believe that, not for one single second."
Picking his nose and wiping it underneath the seat

Text messages Ada has sent Natalie's boyfriend Rex from the airport

Thanks again for taking care of things while we're gone. Just a heads up – Sir Richard likes to kick litter out of the box. The broom and dustpan are behind the utility door. Pls. stack the mail on Kevin's desk in his office. Send us an e-mail if something comes up. Thanks!

??

Oh no! Which one?

<sigh> Sweep up all the glass, pls

Kevin's first marriage

Cammie had an extensive snow globe collection, fourteen in total. She made a point of buying a new one every time they went on vacation. For years, the snow globes were stored in the garage but recently Kevin asked Ada if she would mind if he displayed them again. She said of course she didn't mind in a tone of voice that made clear the snow globes should stay in his office.

In photographs, Cammie emanates a sensible prettiness, her clothes comfortable-looking, a cursory nod to style. After Cammie died, Kevin's mom told him to be thankful it happened quickly. She said, *Some people drag out death like it's poker game with a cash prize at the end.*

Killed instantly, the police officer told Kevin, who had been at home with the girls, the three of them waiting patiently for Cammie to return home from the grocery store with milk.

What everyone is studiously avoiding saying on this trip

Cammie died on Ada's birthday. She was forty.

A conversation between Ada and Kevin before they married

"Do you want me to take your last name?"

"I don't care about stuff like that."

"Really?"

"It's your name."

"Did you ask Cammie to change her name?"

"I didn't ask her to. I think it was something she wanted to do."

"I changed my name with Thomas, so it seems like I should change it this time. Although maybe that's bad luck. But if you want me to change it, I will. If it's important to you."

"It's not important to me."

"You won't say in a few years that you wish I had changed it, or imply that I should have known that it mattered to you, and that even though you're saying it's fine *now*, you'll be secretly, or not so secretly, disappointed *then*?"

"Why would I do that?"

(long pause)

"I have a hard time believing you really don't have an opinion one way or the other about whether I take your name."

"But it's your name, not mine."

"That's the part I'm struggling with."

Text messages Natalie's boyfriend Rex has sent Ada from the house

Ur cat brke a snoq glow Srry ☹

snob glome

SNOW GLOBE

Idk

Ada's first marriage

At month-three of their marriage, Thomas told Ada he was also in love with Karen, Ada's stepsister. The *also* part was confusing, although Thomas, in his defense, did try to explain. He said he did love her (Ada) but he also loved her (Karen) and that if he hadn't loved her (Ada) he wouldn't have married her. He had assumed that after getting married to Ada, his feelings for Karen would fade and eventually disappear, like a food stain on a favorite shirt. Later he would regret this analogy because of the way Ada latched onto it. What kind of stain? Which sister was the favorite shirt?

In photographs from his and Ada's wedding, Thomas has a shifty-eyed look about him that is noticeable even to people who don't know the whole story. Karen later told Ada's mother this was mostly due to cataracts.

Ada was sitting on their gray couch when Thomas first told her he was also in love with Karen. This discussion would happen many times over the next few months, in various rooms of the house and, occasionally, in public. Certain phrases would be repeated, other words swallowed up. As Thomas talked that first morning, snow fell. The flurries became fat, blurred flakes as he repeated words like *infatuation, my real self,* and *I don't know.* The conversation – best to call it a monologue – started when Ada asked, "Do you want more coffee while I'm up?"

Fights Kevin and Ada had their third year of marriage

Whether the burden of cleaning the litter box should always fall to the same person

If it's okay to say "Well, so are you" when a twelve-year-old girl calls you a bitch

The fairness of asking someone to stop wearing a favorite sweater because it reminds the other person of a sweater someone else used to wear

Whether fight number 3 is a reason to attend marriage counseling

Kevin and Cammie's last conversation

Kevin: Where are you going?

Cammie: Grocery store. We're out of milk and the girls want hot chocolate.

Kevin: I bought a gallon yesterday.

Cammie: You bought regular milk.

Kevin: I thought I bought organic.

Cammie: I just looked – it's regular. I'm taking your car because mine is low on gas.

Kevin: Fine.

Cammie: I told the girls to clean up the art stuff in the playroom when I'm gone.

Kevin: Okay.

Cammie: Be back soon.

Kevin: Drive safely. Love you.*

    * things he didn't say

Times Kevin has called Ada "Cammie" and Ada has called him "Thomas"

Cooking dinner

Giving directions in the car

"Could you answer that, Thomas?"

"Hey Cam, where are the beach towels?"

Similarities between Kevin and Ada's first husband Thomas
Both are, scientifically speaking, the heterogametic sex because of their two distinct sex chromosomes (XY)
Both have two vowels in his first name
Both dislike the nubby blue nightgown Ada sleeps in when she's sick

What is written in very small letters on the back wall of the handicapped stall in Terminal 2 near Gate A7 where Ada is hiding and eating peanut M&Ms
You guys, stop wearing white after Labor Day!

A letter from Karen three years ago
Karen compared Ada's hurt and anger over her divorce (with Thomas) and Karen's marriage six months later (to Thomas) to the kidney stones she (Karen) used to get as a teenager. Best for Ada to release those toxic feelings lest they calcify inside her and require endoscopic blasting. Ada memorized the line, *All scars, no matter how ugly or raised, become ordinary in time.* It would have been nicer if Karen had added that scars become less ordinary when seen by someone new. Even better: forgetting you even have a scar, until you catch sight of it unexpectedly. Oh right, you say. *That.*

In photographs, Karen has a slightly stunned expression, large deep-set eyes, a rosebud mouth.

I so wish it hadn't turned out this way, Karen wrote. *In case you're thinking I'm a selfish person who doesn't give a whit about other people's feelings.*

The letter reminded Ada that Karen had briefly

considered a career in theater.

The letter's P.S. was an invitation for Ada, Kevin, and the girls (referred to in the letter as *your family*) to visit Karen, Thomas, and their son Chai (referred to in the letter as *my family*) in Phoenix.

A week before the trip, Ada ripped up the letter into tiny pieces and flushed it down the toilet. The night before the trip, Ada broke out in hives and spent the night vomiting in the bathroom. The next morning, her family brought her toast and hot tea. Those two days Ada spent in bed were referred to as *that godawful stomach bug you had*.

The airport gift shop

The shop is empty except for Ada and the owner of the store. He's wearing a stiff cowboy hat and a t-shirt that reads APA EAR in white block letters on the front.

Prominently displayed in the middle of the store is that book everyone is reading and urging others to read. It's one of those books where lovers are miraculously reunited after decades apart. In this particular novel, the reunion takes place on a cruise ship heading to Antarctica. Even though Ada stopped reading books like this years ago, she picks it up and reads a page from the middle: *I think of you every hour of every day.*

She laughs out loud.

"I can't keep that book in stock," Cowboy Hat says.

"I'm not surprised," Ada says.

She wanders over to the snow globes: a cow kneeling between two catcti, two orange squirrels cavorting in a desert, a deer sniffing a pair of rainbow-colored cowboy boots. A small shake sends glitter raining down on the cow, snow into the desert, confetti into the deer's eyes.

Ada puts a pack of gum and the cow snow globe on the counter. "What's 'apa ear'?"

"It used to say Papa Bear," Cowboy Hat says. He traces the ghost letters with his index finger. "Present from my son. He's twenty now." He tosses the snow globe into a bag along with a few sheets of newspaper. "You'll want to wrap that up."

Ada unwraps a piece of gum at the counter. "Our flight's delayed," she says to Cowboy Hat. "The flight time is listed in red."

He raises his eyebrows, tips his hat. "My condolences."

Text messages Natalie has sent Rex from the airport
Actually, Natalie has not sent Rex any text messages.

On the occasion of the flight time suddenly turning green
Cashmere Sock Knitting lady stands up and claps. There is a communal hesitation, a weighty pause as the other passengers look at each other and then at Cashmere Sock lady. The question looms large: is this event worthy of a standing ovation? It's unclear who joins in first but within seconds, all of gate A7, minus Natalie, joins in. A sudden manic joy fills the boarding area. Kevin leans down and kisses Ada and she kisses him back with an exuberance that starts off silly but eventually is real.

As everyone lines up to board, the flight attendants pass out free drink tickets. Natalie pockets hers and meets Ada's gaze. "What?" she asks. Her defiance has a ring of innocence that makes Ada feel unexpectedly tender.

Ada holds out her hand, and Natalie slaps the drink ticket into her hand. "Happy early birthday, A."

PRESTI/DIGITING

Kanya Kanchana

"Sit here. Watch carefully now."

It was just last week. I sat at this table right here. I watched like she told me to, i.e., carefully. First, she put an old plate (aluminium, dinged) on the table, and upon it, an egg (chicken, white).

"It's an egg," I said.

"Crack it." I cracked it. It had another shell right inside the first one. My teeth went on edge. I slid off the chair.

"Wait, there's more." She removed the egg and put another (same chicken) in its place. It quivered like jelly. It had no shell whatsoever, just the membrane.

What? What *what*? My teeth were bared now. She smiled a slim one.

. . .

"Do you want to see something cool?"

"Mm-hm."

She lay down on the floor and bared her belly (flat, smooth). Three fingerwidths above the navel, she placed a one-rupee coin (solid, copper-nickel). Took a deep breath and exhaled. A crease formed beneath the coin and trapped it. Inhaled. The coin flipped over. My eyes grew wide.

Exhale. Standing coin. Inhale. Flipping coin. My cheeks burned. Exhale. Inhale.

The coin was far below her belly button now. I touched my belly. Then I ran away.

"Don't run too far. The banjaras are coming later this afternoon. You'll want to be around." I heard her laughing.

belly

Juliana Lamy

belly

Juliana Lamy

When she disappears on purpose, the only thing Auntie Farrah leaves for Arbor is a black-and-white composition book. Auntie Farrah's already shown her how to divide her life up into wedges, hand them out like orange slices to the things they make from the mud of the creek behind the house. There's this free pottery-making class downtown that Arbor's been taking almost since she could sit up on her own, and she's worked with the river mud before. She knows how to make things.

But she's never made a person before.

It doesn't take long for her to give the diagram a try. It's always just been the two of them, and Arbor's not too keen on staying in the house by herself, especially when she has a choice. There's this sort of sticky loneliness that webs everything together after Farrah's gone, gums them to each other like it's trying to make sure nothing else gets out. Arbor leaves for work with it on her clothes; it makes her legs feel too heavy on the carpet when she's driving her truck, like the bottom of her shoes are lined with Velcro.

For the next few weeks, she works. There are a lot of diagrams in the composition book Auntie Farrah leaves her, ones that focus on building legs and arms and ears. They stretch and twist the body like it's something to be crumpled between pages. It—*that*—makes her so uncomfortable that she duct-tapes the journal to the wall above the headboard of the bed she works on, keeps it open so that each appendage is given some stillness. It's Auntie Farrah's room, free space now.

She works till her back aches and her eyes water, till pops of dirt touch down on her forearms like a reckless mist, like bits of a nighttime dark chipped straight from the source. When she falls asleep on the floor, because she hardly sleeps in her own bed these days, the taste of the mud is so heavy in her mouth that she wakes up coughing. She misses her hotel management class, but she knows there are about two months left of the semester, and this—she wants to do this.

It takes her almost a month to build out its torso, the beginning of its thighs, its arms and shoulders. Sometimes she has to break off finished pieces and re-do them. She skips the curve between its legs, unsure. Her cheeks burn.

There is something nobody tells you about giving someone a face. That their nose, their lips, the bones in their cheeks, will be ragged scraps clinking down onto the tile under your feet from the splintering mental scenes of people you can barely remember, the dislocated anchors of people-based dreams that you wouldn't recognize as yours even if someone played a whole film reel of them for you.

Arbor gives her friend a wide forehead, and she thinks she's seen a woman with one just like it at the downtown Walmart before, but there's no way to be sure. The face is lumpy and one eye is bigger than the other, but it is not misshapen. She doesn't know how to make hair from the mud, and there are no instructions in her Auntie's book, so she doesn't try it. She checks the fingers again, the toes, makes sure that they're long enough.

Arbor finishes in the middle of the day. A Sunday that makes her feel misplaced, like she should be at church even though she probably hasn't been since she was a baby (Auntie Farrah once told her that her birth parents were Methodists). Auntie Farrah used to tell Arbor that she didn't like how wobbly it all was, how there was nothing tight or solid about a connection with somebody or something that you could only get at with one-sided singing and shouting. And Auntie Farrah never thought that the prayers did anything but ping around in your own head, raw peas bouncing against an aluminum bowl.

Arbor pulls back to look at her finished friend. One of her ankles bends outwards, like the crooked leg of a bobby pin.

She has to wake them up now. Auntie Farrah wrote all about that, too, in the first pages of the journal. You don't need much to wake up something that doesn't need to breathe—Auntie Farrah taught Arbor how to make her own clay toys when she was little, tiny bears and dogs and dragons that would chase her up and down the hall until Auntie called her in to get her hair braided. They were more like wind-up toys, like those jack-in-the-boxes or those spinning ballerinas—nothing but movement. They don't need much of you, just the piece of your consciousness and your life that you decide to give.

Auntie Farrah told her that she's no guest in her own body, she lives in it and it's hers. And Arbor started to think of herself as a packed house with something wild and sharp and life-giving in every corner. She could wake up those breathless things with the plaster from the roof of her mouth, the flakes of tile tucked into her nailbeds, the electrical wires jumbling gorgeous around themselves right out of her scalp.

But the directions in the journal Auntie Farrah leaves her talk about something else. Talk about feeling a body shift and pull under you as its chest get swollen with brand-new breath. Feeling it warm itself, its blood a stovetop fire, as the clay smooths out and softens into skin.

And the book tells her that it's not just a psychic thing. She can't just *imagine* breaking off pieces of herself to share. It embarrasses her, reading about the physical tokens you use to bring a body to life—piss and mucous and other things she skips over because she can't stand to read them out, even within the deadbolted quiet of her own head.

But there's spit, too. She can do that one.

She puts a knee on the bed and leans forward over her friend, tries to ignore how uncomfortably the plastic bag that she'd laid out on the bed clings to her sweaty thigh. Gives saliva seconds to well up under the thick ledge of her tongue. And as it's dripping past her lips onto her friend's chin, she decides to think of it as water because that's easier. Because she likes the Arbor-manufactured personal truth that there's some buried ocean in the neighborhood of her spine, that the wet frothy beads sliding across her friend's closed eyelids are nothing but the spin-offs of a geyser, pluming hot and barely solid up her throat because the magma in her stomach has set the water in her core to a manic boil.

Arbor doesn't know what she expects—maybe for their eyes to pop open like they're on some NBC soap-opera, waking up from a coma to find out that their father is really their brother—but nothing happens. Their face is still, and Arbor's saliva is drying.

She leaves the room, showers with the water so cold each hit of it snatches at her back like the beak of some pliers. She checks her phone for any calls from unknown numbers. Auntie Farrah has never had a phone—she's always been one of those people that can just sit on news, rapture-good or broken bone-bad—but she could call from a payphone or somebody else's line. It could happen, so Arbor always checks.

It's when Arbor's dressed in her sleep clothes and walking towards the kitchen to grab some water that she hears it. Three sneezes that sound just like the muted rasp of those blow-darts Arbor's seen kids use to spear iguanas at the pier. Then a heavy groan.

"Ughhh, is this—is this spit?"

When Arbor walks in, slow, her friend is sitting up on the bed. And they're not a talking clay-mold, nothing out of a stop-motion animated feature. That's what Arbor had been expecting. That's what her toys always were, what the cups and bowls that Auntie Farrah liked to keep (Farrah always seemed to find it funny) always were. And of course the book had said that the exterior cast would stretch itself out into skin. *Real* skin, flecked with pores that would make it look like some careful, obsessive sketch artist dappled it in pen ink. Arbor definitely hadn't made those dots. So where'd they come from?

When they turn to look at Arbor, her alarm chews away at her heavy shock so well that she finds her feet light enough to run out of the room. She ignores the impulse though, even when it tells her, "Hey, you would *definitely* make it down the street in about twenty seconds if you sprinted out of here right now."

There's no white in her friend's eyes. They're nothing but ill-lit amber iris, the color of an avocado pit. Their face is normal, jaw just a little too sharp but in that pretty way no one ever seems to mind. Arbor has no idea how she ever managed to get their head that perfectly round.

It feels painful in a bizarre sort of way, to be under somebody else's eyes again. Like her muscles are working overtime to make her worth seeing, cords in her back pulling her up tight to stand straight, calves fighting against her knock-knees. It's nothing like when she delivers the mail or goes to the class she audits. It's not even like when she drops off Cherif Hidalgo's packages, and he walks out of his house with his robe half open and a too-wide smile on his face for her. She's sore under this look.

Her friend narrows their eyes at her. "Did you spit on me?"

Before Arbor can answer that they're already on to the next thing, staring down the line of their body, down past their flat chest and towards the curve between their legs. They reach for it with a hand and Arbor looks away.

"Good choice," they say, still doing what they're doing. "I like not being defined by anything yet. Although I kind of want a name. Do I have one?"

Arbor looks back at them. "No, I—I couldn't think of anything."

They're smiling a little bit, and Arbor sees that their teeth are white as naked sea salt. How does that work?

"Oh come on! I'm sure you can think of something."

Arbor thumbs through some memories, relieved when her mind settles on something. The barest scene from a *Days of Our Lives* rerun.

"Lee? How's Lee?"

Her friend leans against the headboard, thinks for a moment.

"I like it! It's definitely not like one of those place names, like America or India." Are they baiting her? Arbor's confused. They look at her for a moment. "You have a place name, don't you." It's not a question.

"It's Arbor."

Lee laughs. "Why'd they leave out the 'Ann' and the 'Michigan?' Could've thrown in a zip code too to really stick the landing."

Arbor doesn't want to rise to it, but she can't help herself. It's been so long since somebody clowned her. She's out of practice.

"What's wrong with place names?"

"They're corny. The minute you name a set of buildings, the name's dead. Pick something else."

It sounds like something Arbor might say, if she was braver with herself. It feels a bit like Lee is tickling at the back of her mind, drawing out the things that would never leave her mouth. It makes Arbor pause, confused. The journal hadn't said anything about a mental connection, and it certainly doesn't *feel* like there's somebody else riding passenger's-side in her head.

Arbor's not quite sure *what* to do. On the one hand, it fucking worked! She molded the mud and followed Auntie Farrah's instructions and now the outturn is sitting up in bed, talking to her. Getting on her nerves a little, sure, but talking to her.

"Do you want something to wear?"

Lee laughs again. "No. But you can go ahead and throw me whatever you have, if you want."

When Lee gets up from the bed, Arbor notices that they have a limp because of their crooked ankle. She tries not to let it stick with her, but it does, raps at her like knuckles on a jangling iron fence. *Look what you did.*

They're a little short, too, although Arbor's hardly one to talk. She'd stopped growing at fourteen, still gets carded for Nyquil sometimes.

Lee waits for her to leave the room, like she means to follow her, but Arbor hesitates. Lee rolls their fruit-pit eyes.

"I'm not gonna jump on your back and ram you into a wall, *relax* a little." Oddly specific. When Arbor doesn't say anything or move, a little too unnerved to do either, Lee walks ahead of her. Stops, looks back at her over their shoulder. "Tell me where to go."

Arbor gives them the first things she can find, a black night shirt with this logo of a laughing dolphin wearing bowling shoes, so big it hangs to mid-thigh on them. A pair of sweats from the laundry basket in front of her bed. She gives them blankets and they leave. She doesn't even check to see where they've decided to sleep, Auntie Farrah's room or someplace else. Arbor can barely sleep herself.

■　■　■

She didn't go to the police when Auntie Farrah disappeared. She doesn't know if that makes her a bad niece yet. The day Auntie Farrah left she took all her stuff with her. Arbor mostly thinks she went somewhere on her own, but—she doesn't know.

Plus, there are plenty of things she's seen Cherif Hidalgo do that make it more likely she'd eat the metal piping in her walls before she ever asked him for help. One of them scratches at her all the time, Brillo-pad-rough.

Before it came out that the owners were selling codeine from the basement, the Corner Cafe was one of the biggest spots in Cypress.

When she watched Cherif Hidalgo make a dangerous ass of himself, she was ten.

She and Auntie Farrah were leaving the Cafe and heading to their car. There was this group of kids a little ways away from where Auntie Farrah had parked, in a part of the lot that was mostly empty. They were teenagers, definitely older than her. The final spurts of daylight that gushed past powerlines and tree branches found them where they stood laughing, listening to something with a tick-tocking Caribbean pulse (and this isn't to generalize; it's whatever sits underneath Jamaican and Haitian and Puerto Rican music that cooks it into something anyone raised on the sound of a guitar or a marimba or a tcha tcha would recognize). Daylight broke into the kids wherever it could—the thin skin at the shell of their ears, the tops of their cheeks—and lit them up till everyone there, from kids deep brown like Coca Cola in its glass bottle to kids copper brown like pennies, looked like they rose in the east and set in the west.

Cherif Hidalgo came from behind the Cafe's mini playground section, rounded the duck-shaped seesaw where it stood hushed and un-moving on one coiled leg. He was in Bermuda shorts and flip-flops, already stroking the gun at his hip like it was the head of some big cat. Arbor thinks he was waiting for a sandpaper tongue to ease out of the barrel to lick at his fingers. It was always with him then, like it is now. She and Auntie Farrah used to see him all the time at the Cafe, when they went. He'd put the gun on the table next to his food. One time, she even saw him mistake it for a napkin. They were sitting close enough for Arbor to see how the handle came away sticky with pancake syrup.

His jaw was already tight when he walked up to the group. He spoke to exactly one person. A boy with deep brown dreads that rolled across his back with each breath he took, had Arbor thinking of those long candles they use in the dinner scenes of every Christmas movie.

They couldn't have spoken for more than two minutes before Cherif Hidalgo was wrenching his gun from its holster. The boy, and everyone else, jerked back.

"Why can't you listen?" Arbor only heard it because he yelled it. "Why can't you listen?"

He shot at the ground at their feet. The teenagers were far away enough, that part of the lot empty enough, that it didn't hit any of them. Only bounced back and caught Cherif Hidalgo in the leg. The first time she ever heard the word "motherfucker," in a screech packed up with pain, was when Cherif Hidalgo fell down from the hurt and shock of his self-inflicted bullet wound. Auntie Farrah was already pulling her away, pulling her back, as Arbor told her (because her auntie *needed* to know),

"Auntie, he's bleeding wrong."

He had to be. In the TV shows she used to watch in secret, after Auntie Farrah went to bed, the blood came out hard and mad when somebody got shot. But Cherif Hidalgo's blood came out thin and shy, trickled down his leg in these cords that looked like red drawstrings.

Auntie Farrah almost lifted her up off the ground, trying to get the both of them back to their car as fast as she could. But Arbor saw it. He shot some more, shaky, like the gun was bucking in his hands. He hit the seesaw duck right between the eyes as they drove away.

Sometimes Arbor still dreams about that. Auntie Farrah throwing her arms around her, holding her close, towing Arbor away with her.

■ ■ ■

Arbor's work days start early. Of course, she has an alarm clock, but it's usually her next door neighbor's Nutribullet that wakes her, the round grinding sound that wheels itself right out of Miss Dawn's kitchen and into her room. Auntie Farrah used to have one just like it but Arbor broke it years ago when she tried to blend her mini-Snickers bars into chocolate juice.

Usually Miss Dawn's NutriBullet wakes the woman's baby which wakes her Terrier and then Arbor's up, watching the sun pick past sleepy clouds to take its seat for the day.

But today, it's a sound like splitting glass that yanks Arbor loose from sleep. Her clock reads six a.m., a whole hour before she, Miss Dawn, and the baby are usually up. She's scrambling out of bed half-awake still, almost crashes headfirst into her TV.

As she's rushing down the hall there is another sound, too, one that dribbles in through her ears wet, like something big and invisible is drooling it into her. It leaks through till her head is full of it and the inside of her skull is caked with it, reminds her of old, leftover batter against the sides of a mixing bowl. It is high, impossible to miss, two steps down from what she assumes a dog whistle sounds like to dogs. But it's restless. It has hitches, and variations, and—hiccups?

Is that crying?

When she gets to the kitchen, she can't quite make sense

of what she's seeing, not all at once. Her head catalogues the scene element by element like rungs on a ladder: there are pieces of dark broken glass on the blue checker-print linoleum, scattered around the legs of the breakfast table. A whole box of Cinnamon Toast Crunch is tipped over on the counter, bits of cereal shaped like keyboard keys streaming onto the floor. Lee is kneeling on the counter, looking down at Arbor with wide eyes and their hand still clutching the knob of a vertical cabinet's door.

After big hurricanes down here every conscious thing's mind is chafed to hell, on-edge. In the wake of them there, would be these strange sounds in their backyard that Arbor and her aunt would investigate themselves because the power lines were down and all their neighbors were busy enough re-orienting post storm. More often than not, those sounds would turn out to be squirrels, just as rattled about the fallen trees in their backyard as they were. Auntie Farrah's electric lamp would catch them in a palpitating, warped disk of loud white light, and their eyes would look all the bigger for it. That's what Lee looks like right now.

"Uhh—good morning? I got hungry, but I didn't want to wake you up and—"

Arbor doesn't know how she's been ignoring it this long. The sharp ringing sound is still going, even stronger now that she's in the kitchen and—oh shit, she's an idiot. She gets closer to the broken shards near the table, kneels down and picks them up. Feels it while she hears it, the *squealing crying irritation* and a slight thudding ache that spreads through her palms, reminds her of what a tooth feels like when it needs to be pulled out.

"Is that sound—that's them?"

"Yeah," Arbor says, shifting the shards around a bit

in her hands. "Stuff like this happens when it dries as clay—they're actually pretty fragile, just like mugs from a store."

Arbor hears shifting, and soon Lee is kneeling down next to her, staring down into her hand. They look up at her, eyes still wide.

"You can fix it though, right?"

Arbor raises a brow at them, shifts the shards around meaningfully. "Uhm? You see this, yeah?"

Lee rolls her eyes, and Arbor's stuck on the movement. So fluid, natural. Amazing.

"I'm not asking you to whip out a roll of Scotch tape and get to sticking. I'm just—like, you know how to do stuff like this. So you can fix it."

Arbor frowns, considering. She's never tried to do anything like that before. When her mud toys broke, Auntie Farrah would just throw them away and let her make more. But then again, they'd never screeched like this. Maybe if she brought the pieces back to the river? But—

"I have work soon."

"Have a heart Ann Arbor!"

"What I'm *trying* to have is a house to live in. I can't just blow this off." Arbor doesn't mention that her shift doesn't even start for another hour. The river's only about a fifteen-minute walk into the woods behind them.

Lee squints at her. "So when's the screaming gonna stop? When one of your neighbors calls in about the Corgi you're torturing in your kitchen? You know when white people think you're fucking with a dog, they'd run you into the ocean in their Crocs if they could. And the cops they summon would barely be able to stop themselves from helping."

Arbor's stunned again. She was in too much shock last night to *really* think about it, but now she remembers how Lee had mentioned India and America and Michigan so casually, like it was nothing.

"How do you know all of that?"

Lee frowns. "All of what? Stop stalling."

Lee's fruit-pit eyes still make Arbor feel like there's a draft coming in through a half-open door somewhere, catching her at the back of her neck. She's looking at their smooth bald head when she says yes.

Arbor wraps the pieces up in the thickest towel she can find at the back of her closet, to muffle the noise. Watches Lee where they're standing right outside her bedroom door with a regular bowl full of milk and cereal, munching away while they wait for Arbor. Watches the thin fingers of their hand shift smoothly to grip the handle of their spoon and remembers when she'd made them, when they were just static, drying mud. Something clogs her throat. She's ashamed. She goes to Lee.

"Hold this," she says, barely gives them enough time to grab the bundle before she's heading back to the kitchen.

She climbs onto the counter and throws the cabinet doors open, looks for the other bowls and cups. She finds them, puts them down next to her so she can clamber back to the floor.

"There were more."

Arbor swallows as she grabs a trash bag, starts to pile them in.

"Uh-huh."

"That's so weird, you guys just—kept them? And ate from them?"

Arbor doesn't like Lee's voice. "I never did."

Before Lee can say anything else Arbor's taking the bundle from them, grasping the garbage bag tight, and power-walking to the back door. Nudging a pair of sandals in Lee's direction.

Lee doesn't say anything the whole walk there. Arbor breaks off into a set of thick trees, and it's only Lee's steps behind her crushing dead leaves and twigs, just barely out-of-sync with her own like they're actually a single thing walking and time is just lagging, that let her know they're still there. It makes Arbor feel like she's caught up in the center of a prolapsing moment, like the seconds skid from lane to lane so fast that sometimes they actually roll over themselves, make present people plop down onto future people plop down onto folks from the past. She doesn't like it.

It's an easy path, even though there's no distinguishable trail. So it's impossible for Arbor to ignore how, right now, Lee is nothing but a moving silence at her back, thick through with blood and flesh but quiet all the same.

They get to the river and it is as beautiful as it always is. Fast and foaming, rushing noisy while pear-green frogs hop and play next to it.

Being in the mud feels just like it always does—like she's in the company of a boundless, unfenced light, something just like those beams that sprawl across the savanna of space till they hit the hard curve of a planet and have no choice but to stop. When Arbor shares herself, she is the hard curve. Light is nothing but pure energy, after all. She has to gift it something from the house of her, condense it into something living. That's how this happens.

Arbor crouches down and unwraps the towel first, lays it across her thighs while she takes up the pieces, careful as anything. She feels ashamed again. Why did Auntie Farrah ever find this funny? To keep these things like this?

She doesn't turn back to look at Lee once as she does it, just tucks all the shards into the mud, and then the cups and bowls she brought too. For a moment, all of the objects just sit on the surface. Then they sink, like stones in water, until the mud is just as even as Arbor had found it. She swallows.

When Arbor does look back, Lee's still there, perched on a big rock near the drop curtain of the trees. Like she doesn't want to come too close to the mud. Probably for the best, Arbor thinks.

But they're smiling.

.　■　.

Arbor's in a good mood for work that day but of course it doesn't last.

Arbor's not afraid to say it, okay? (Well, to anyone but her boss). She's skipped Cherif Hidalgo's house before on her route, when he was lounging on his porch shirtless or watering his plants in a robe way too short for her liking.

And she has *every* intention of doing it again, but he's complained about her to her supervisor twice already. If she skips him again, they'll suspend her.

She knows what kind of man Cherif Hidalgo is. Recognizes that he's more lenient with her than she's ever seen him be with anyone else. It leaves a sour taste in her mouth.

She gets out of the truck and stuffs his mail into the receptacle at the front of his lawn, three regular letters and some lumpy, misshapen thing wrapped up in pineapple-yellow packaging. His lawn is still empty, so far so good.

But as Arbor is still struggling with the last parcel, she hears the front door open. When she looks up, he's in a paper-thin shower robe that makes her think of a hospital gown worn backwards. He's wearing a gold chain, and his chest hair curls over it like it's trying to get a good grip, like at any moment at all it might snap it from his neck. He looks like a Dollar Store pimp.

She notices something dangling out of his robe, limp against his leg.

He grins at her with teeth white as limestone.

"I missed you, love. Will you drink with me today?"

Arbor's pretty sure she trips back into the driver's seat of her truck in her rush to get away. She thinks about it all day, and if she could, she wouldn't leave the truck for the rest of shift. Just toss everybody's shit onto their walkways and wish them the best of luck with it. Like she's done with Cherif Hidalgo before.

. . .

She's not sure what she expects to find when she comes back to the house after work.

Miss Dawn's younger brother Orion used to live in town before he took up this nude calendar modelling gig in New York. When Arbor was around nine or ten, he'd ride down their street on this neon-blue motorcycle, engine snarling loud enough to scare the soul out of anybody within a half-mile radius. The sound used to grate on Farrah's nerves so much she would end her dominoes games with Arbor early, go off to watch TV or crochet. And her Auntie worked such long hours at the Steakhouse uptown. Arbor only really got to see her during mud-making and dominoes. So one day, when they were sitting at the kitchen table with the pieces laid out between them, Arbor got up just as she heard the growing sound of the motorcycle engine getting closer. Got the front door open before her Auntie could do much of anything and ran out into the middle of the street.

She stood there. Doesn't remember being scared, just irritated. The bike came careening down the road towards her, stopped so close to her she could feel its hot breath on her bare legs like a panting thing. The rider had tight curly hair and a square jaw.

"Do you always gotta be that loud?" she'd wanted to know.

And he'd laughed, straight gleaming teeth where she could see, like they were old friends. When she got back into the house Auntie Farrah made her promise she'd never do anything like that again, her mouth pulled into a line as hard and straight across as a median strip.

Orion left for New York a few days later. Arbor was coming home from school when she'd seen him loading some suitcases into the bed of Miss Dawn's Chevy. He'd waved to her before he got in the passenger's seat.

A lot of people think that because Arbor's quiet, that means she's careful. Auntie Farrah knew better, knew that reckless was always easier to find when it's noisy, but you've gotta look for it all the same, every time.

So Arbor's kicking herself a little bit for leaving Lee, a perfect stranger barely a day old, alone in her house. When she gets inside, she half-expects fires in every room, ripped up wall-paper—maybe Lee's fallen apart somehow like the bowl from this morning and that makes her anxious enough to shove through the door.

She hears the *Sanford and Son* theme song blaring

louder than it's ever played from the center of the house.
The volume must be on the highest setting. When she
follows the song she sees Redd Foxx reading a newspaper
in his rocking chair on screen but the living room is empty.
So is Farrah's room, when she goes to check.

She finds Lee perched on the edge of her bed with
a textbook on their lap. They shift, and Arbor notices
that it's the copy of *Hospitality Management: How to Keep
'Em Coming Back* she'd bought to make her feel like she
wasn't just pretending when she went to the class at the
community college. Arbor tries to find something to say
about what happened this morning—maybe it'll even
land her at some sort of apology—but Lee speaks up first.
She taps on the book with a finger.

"You know if you let me stay in one of these places, I
wouldn't break your shit fixing breakfast."

Arbor's not sure Lee's joking but she laughs anyway.

"Are you kidding? If I could afford that shit at all, *I'd*
get a room for myself, stick *you* with this house and the—"

Arbor stops. She was about to say something about
Cherif Hidalgo from this morning, but she lets it spill
back down her throat. Lee picks up her slack.

"You could really leave this house like that?"

Arbor shrugs before she can really think about it. "'S
just a house."

"Hotels are better?"

"Sure."

"I read something in here about how some hotel dining
rooms have a capacity of like four-hundred people. I'm
not sure how much you'd like sitting elbow to elbow and
getting somebody else's lip sweat in your yogurt but if
that's what you're into—"

Arbor rolls her eyes. "Lee. I like hotels to manage.

Manage. Not to live in."

Lee narrows their eyes at her. "Maybe I don't know what *manage* means. You're already talking down to me, guess you're a natural at this authority thing."

"So you *do* know what it means."

"Why do you want to manage hotels?"

Arbor isn't sure how to answer the question. She's never had to before. Auntie Farrah worked at the Marriott a few towns over for a year, before they found asbestos in the walls and the whole thing had to be torn down. She'd come home smelling like vanilla perfume and lemon tea, even though she hated smelling like anything at all. It made Arbor think of a full place, with bodies leaning over banisters and squeezing through dining rooms so restless that the hard-sharp edge of the tables would jam bruises into their thighs, sloping in against each other so tight that skin held scent like memory. Where the sudden absence of one person was an empty cramping belly for nothing but a few moments, never for long. Glass sliding doors swallowed them in like bread.

"I'm good with people when all I have to do is listen to them."

Lee looks right at her, and Arbor gets that overwhelming urge to look away again, sharp draft at the back of her neck.

"That's a two-person thing, huh."

Arbor shrugs again.

■ ■ ■

The next few weeks are good. Real good. It seems like everyday that Arbor comes home from work or her hotel class or her pottery sessions, Lee is fixated on some other activity. There's a day when Arbor finds them on the carpet in front of the TV in a handstand, some yoga infomercial playing across the screen. She comes home the next day with a bright purple exercise mat that she'd picked up from the sporting goods' store on her route. Lee laughs and tells her that they're "impressed that she could talk to somebody else out loud for that long instead of just combusting when they couldn't read her mind." Arbor threatens to take the mat back, and Lee tells her they'd sooner take the hands off her wrists.

Arbor finds them on the couch with Auntie Farrah's old crocheting supplies, has to bite back her impulse to rip them from their hands. Especially when they look up at her grinning.

Arbor finds them with her computer on their lap, about thirteen different tabs open to astrology pages. Her laptop's password-protected and she changes it every month. That's when she starts to really wonder: exactly how much of herself did she give to Lee when she woke them up?

Apparently, she's a Pisces sun but an Aries moon.

"You get mad, but it's under, like, plastic wrap," Arbor explains.

"I thought Pisces was a water sign?"

"Shut the fuck up."

Things are real good.

So when Arbor comes home from class three weeks later to an empty house, it feels like there's an anvil sitting on her chest. It comes back to her like she's still in the middle of it, that day when she'd walked into Farrah's room to find nothing but a sheetless mattress. When she'd thrown open every single door to every single room in that house as quickly as she could, afraid that if she didn't barge in fast enough, she'd miss her, and her auntie would escape through a window or an air vent.

She hears a door open and close as she's sitting on the closed lid of her toilet, trying to do something about the lead in her chest. She feels her bones clinking like keys in her skin with the sudden noise.

She rushes out to the back door to see Lee, taking off their shoes.

"Where'd you go?"

"Just down the street." Lee turns to face her, and their eyes widen. "Holy shit, you look like somebody kicked you in the chest and stole your mail truck. Did Miss Dawn's Terrier bite you on the ass again?"

"I thought—" Arbor pauses, tries again. "Somebody could've seen you."

Lee raises a brow. Well, where an eyebrow *would* be if Arbor had ever learned how to make hair with the mud.

"Am I an Area 51 sample or something?" Lee looks at her a bit longer, then brings a hand to their own head and rubs it. "Oooh—is it the bald thing? Maybe I just have alopecia, people don't know."

"Maybe—m-maybe you could wear a wig or something?" Auntie Farrah took all her wigs with her when she left but, "I used to play a lot with my auntie's wigs when I was little. I still have some of them."

Lee sighs, but they agree to it.

Arbor finds her a curly black one that brushes her shoulders. When Lee sees themselves in the standing mirror next to Arbor's door, they say, "It looks like I'm sleeping with the pastor, but I still share the church program with his wife on Sundays."

Arbor can't help but laugh. It strikes a chord too, like it's something she'd probably think but never say, even if there was nobody around but her.

"It looks great."

Arbor gives them a wide navy-colored headband, too, for good measure. It comes down over their brow-ridge and makes them look like they're wearing a bike helmet with the top half popped out. Lee wants to be able to walk all the way to the Exxon that borders their town and Brooksville, their neighbor-town, about two miles out. Arbor chokes on what she actually wants to say—that she'd have Lee to pace back and forth between the house and river fifteen minutes behind them, if she could help it—and they settle on the pier instead, a half mile out. Lee likes to go out in the late afternoons, and Arbor likes it because by then all the neighborhood kids who usually play down there have been snatched back home at the shirt collar by their parents for dinner. They won't get the chance to bother Lee.

The next day, Arbor and the other mail carriers are sorting out their packages at the office after lunch before they resume their routes, and her co-worker Mandy accidentally drops a boxy gray parcel. White dust puffs out from it like chalk from the impact. And things go wild. One minute, Arbor's getting ready to finish out a regular shift. The next, she and everyone else in the building is being escorted out while an alarm that sounds like a sharp pinging, like a fork against a ceramic cup, sounds overhead. They call the police in for the annual anthrax scare. The year before it was just poorly packed baking flour. The year before that it was baby powder that some laundromat owners up in Ocala were using to cut coke, but that news came back to town almost four months after. In the moment everybody in the mailroom just thought somebody was trying to make an under-the-table dollar on toddler rash. Arbor's not complaining as she heads home, not at all.

She's in her sweatpants on the couch, about twenty minutes into that episode of *Good Times* where baby Janet Jackson confesses her love for J.J., when she hears Lee come in from their walk.

"Oh damn, you're home already? I told you the horny old racists down the street could go *one day* without their ValPak coupons."

Lee comes into the living room, stops right in front of the TV because of course they do.

Arbor looks up at them in mock betrayal. "You live to disrespect me." She sees that Lee's holding the gray sweater they'd been wearing this morning in a wrinkled bunch in her hands, just in their white undershirt instead. One sleeve of the jacket is falling over their forearm.

Arbor nods at the roll. "What's that?"

"Oh, I found him when I was down at the pier," Lee tells her, laying the roll down on the coffee table.

When Lee unfolds the jacket, Arbor sees a nuclear green iguana, ugly as sin, laying on its side with its eyes shut. Its skin is the lumpiest thing Arbor's ever seen, looks like it's stretched thin over a whole bunch of chunky gravel pasted together. Dark blood crusts around a small hole in its mint green belly, rings it like a racetrack. Arbor really wants to dive over the back of the couch, scuttle to the kitchen screaming. But she doesn't.

"Lee, what the fuck?"

Lee looks down at her with wide eyes. "What? I figured you could patch him right up and then I can watch you make chicken again while I talk about your cheese string legs. Y'know I'm *pretty* sure you cook better angry anyway—"

Arbor's not squeamish, not really. But who the fuck likes iguanas? She sinks back into the couch a little bit, hopes Lee doesn't notice.

"Lee what do you mean 'fix him up?'"

Lee frowns, uses the edge of a jacket sleeve to poke the thing's stomach. "He's a boy iguana, right? I tried to check, but I'm not *super* sure about figuring out iguana sex."

"No, like," Arbor tries to make her shifting casual as she pulls her legs under her on the sofa, she really does, "what am I fixing?"

Lee sighs, rolls her eyes, like they're tired of having to spell it out for her.

"You can work your weird river magic and bring him back. The baby sociopaths got him in the stomach, *as you can see.*"

Oh. Arbor understands. Lee blinks at her.

"Lee, I can't," her eyes flick to the iguana but it makes her mouth fill up with saliva like she's about to throw up, "I can't bring him back. It doesn't work like that."

Lee frowns again. "But you brought that stuff back to the mud and it just sank in? All the crying and screaming stopped. But it wasn't like they were being suffocated or buried. I saw it, it was like—like healing or something. And me? You woke me up. Just do whatever you did when you woke me up."

"He's not from the river."

"So?"

"So I can't connect to it—" Lee's face hardens at that. "To him. He has to be from the mud, that's the way it is."

Lee is quiet, quiet for a long time.

"Oh," they say.

. . .

Lee buries the iguana out back, kneels down and starts scooping up dirt for a tiny grave before Arbor can get her a spade from the tool shed. They go to bed before Arbor does, for the first time ever.

Laying awake in bed that night because she'd fought hard for sleep and lost, she wonders if Auntie Farrah ever feels her like a phantom limb. Like some arm she lost but didn't lose on the floor of the Clearwater fish processing plant that she'd worked at when Arbor was eleven.

Arbor hears her door creaking open, goes for the bat she always keeps under her bed. But it's Lee.

"I can sleep on the floor."

"You want that?"

Lee snorts. "*You* want that."

Arbor gives them some pillows, some thick comforters to make the hardwood kinder.

It's so quiet again for so long that Arbor thinks Lee's asleep, and Lee probably thinks the same for her. So when Arbor's lips start moving, she doesn't know what the hell it means.

"There's this guy who always has his dick out every time I go to deliver his mail."

Lee makes a choking sound that signals that they're *very* much still awake, something like a scratchy laugh. They sit up. Arbor can barely see their face in the dark.

"You ever try throwing his shit onto the lawn and just driving off instead?"

Arbor laughs. "Yeah. Done it." Then she says, "If my auntie was here, she'd know what to do about it."

"Yeah. Mama Farrah looks like she'd probably bust a few windows for you, in the pics I saw."

That brings Arbor up short. "How do you know her name?"

Lee looks at her. Her eyes are warm, slow honey folding over itself as it's poured into a jar.

"I wouldn't know it unless you wanted me to."

．　．　▪

When Lee finally falls asleep, Arbor's hand falls onto her own stomach. It does it naturally, but it gets her thinking. About hotels and the Corner Cafe and the ugly dead iguana. When she was little Auntie Farrah used to take her with her to volunteer at the soup kitchen downtown every Saturday. She hated it, hated how crowded it got, how loud and smelly, how everyone looked so sad even when they were smiling. She'd only go for her Auntie. So she got real suspicious of herself, thought she was a bad person. Thought that if you carved out her belly-button and brought an eye up to it like a peephole you wouldn't find anything soft inside, nothing but hard, clanking things that caught the light wrong, like old car parts on a back porch under a sun too savage to stop shining.

THE THINGS I TOOK FROM YOUR HOUSE

INNOVATIVE SHORT FICTION CONTEST WINNER

Cassidy McCants

THE THINGS I TOOK FROM YOUR HOUSE

INNOVATIVE SHORT FICTION CONTEST WINNER

Cassidy McCants

- The light blue pillowcase—only because it still smelled of me, somehow. I noticed this day one of dogsitting. I found it funny you had it on Charlotte's pillow and some foreign, frilly thing, must have been hers from adolescence, on yours. Unless you've taken to sleeping on the window side, but this, we both know, would be highly unlikely. Maybe I'm crazy for thinking the shell smelled like me, my hair, after all these years. Maybe it's just that Charlotte and I smell alike. Maybe it's a scent you're drawn to—or, more unsettling for you, always the one in control, maybe it's a scent drawn to you. Though, in college, I remember Charlotte using that organic mint stuff on her hair. Either way, there was no sign, not in the shower, bathroom, garage, recycling, that Charlotte and I use the same shampoo. So I took the case. I can't let you have my scent forever.

- Your book on phenomenology. It's clear it's gone unread for the three years since we parted—enough time for everyone to get over the past, right?—just as it went unread the three we were together. But this one I didn't mean to take. Occasionally, while staying at your place that month, I'd drive over to the cafe nearby and read about perception while feeling guilty for leaving Nelly alone for a couple of hours of our precious time together. I accidentally left the book in my car just before I started packing up to go back to my home, my lackluster and unaffordable downtown apartment. I've been telling myself for two years I'll get a cat, but I just don't believe another creature would be happy in that space with me.

- A stone from Charlotte's antique dresser, which she must have recently painted a bright purple. It was the turquoise stone, all ridges and opacity. I looked it up, and I found it's meant to help maintain serenity, balance. This I took for Charlotte's benefit; she need not depend on rocks to live the life she wants. It's an understandable replacement, stones where God once was for her—has she ever told you the story about her falling, slain in the spirit, at her family's Pentecostal church? I joined her for a service once over winter break, and I was terrified I'd fall too. I shook, shivered, but never fell. Anyway, if anyone needs a wish and a promise for balance, stability, I think it'd be me, the one who's spent a whole month at her ex's marriage home with the dog who used to be her family too. The one who's not sure what kind of alien world she's begun to live in since breaking apart from you. The one who couldn't say no when you asked, even if you only asked for my benefit, out of worry I'm too adrift, unmoored. Think of this one as borrowed from Charlotte—like the many shirts she "borrowed" from me in college, which I always thought was cute. I'll return it one day, years from now.
- My Elvis Costello record. This one speaks for itself—I

found it in its new home, alien among the pristine new-age instrumental albums Charlotte has collected. But I only listened to Charlotte's records during the month at your place. The Zen effects of the more psychedelic-sounding stuff worked pretty well to pass the time on nights when Nelly would go to sleep long before me, her paws outstretched on her new bed, a bed not tattered, the insides strewn all over, like her old one. I'd listen to the tunes, all percussion, or so it seemed. I'd watch Nelly sleep, remember the space she once occupied between us, a space that grew larger and larger as time passed. I remember the realization, years ago, early on, that Nelly would always be there, even when we'd eventually grow distant. I contemplated this alongside the sweeping sounds in your home, an inevitable thought dawning on me: even Nelly, now, though closer than you, had grown faraway from me. She still loved me, just as I will always love her—but I was not, am no longer, integral to her daily life. I suppose she's needed me the past month to feed her, let her out, give her rubs. But she's come to regard me as more of a, say, cool cousin than as a fixture of her immediate family: she breathes heavily, wags her tail, giddy, each time I join her in the living room, the bedroom, the game room. I'm exciting to her now, in a way that makes me feel lonelier than a single stolen piece of turquoise in my pocket.

- From nearby, in the drawer of Charlotte's nightstand, the vibrating wand that looks just like mine, but pink. You always said you give the same gifts over and over. This I didn't want to take; I didn't want to steal her pleasure, the kind I've never been able to get from a man, but after I found myself carefully sanitizing then carefully caressing then carefully cumming on your whiter-than-white bathroom floor, I couldn't in good conscience let her touch the thing again. I keep thinking about a line from the phenomenology book: "Our constant aim is to elucidate the primary function whereby we bring into existence, for ourselves, or take a hold upon, space, the object or the instrument, and do describe the body as the place where this appropriation occurs." I think about how both Charlotte's and my bodies have been appropriated by you.

- The drawing I made for you for Valentine's Day, apparently in 2009. This I found in your shared office, between tattered books and a stack of unused folders. Why was it there? I imagined you and Charlotte staring at the thing, laughing at it, cackling. Charlotte: "Why does the figure look so moody? Lena has never been so melodramatic." Charlotte: "Is that meant to be you, Jack? Is that how she saw you?" Neither of you ever seemed to love my drawings, after all—you were always looking for more color. It can't be good news that this one was out for all to see. I've never felt so belatedly vulnerable. Still, she used to cheer me on. And you used to be my muse. Undue anxiety, I know. You know how I get when it comes to my drawing. I'll never forget your insistence that my work was minimalistic; I'll never forget not voicing that the opposite is what I've always aimed for.
- One of those unused folders, which came to house that drawing, the stone, and
- a photo from your last trip, I'm guessing, to Spain. I know it's strange to take it—the image holds the

two of you, jovial, blissed out, in love. But when we were together, phone cameras just weren't very high-quality. I have similar old photos packed in boxes, confined to Facebook, in silly homemade frames, but in none of them can I see your cheesy Whole Foods smile and dripping amber eyes (I still think they're amber; I wonder if you've come to agree, finally seeing the presence of gold, of honey, the lack of green, brown). I'm glad you have someone who loves you as much as I did—I'm glad you have someone more stable to love after loving a tornado like me. Except for when I'm not glad. One day I'll travel myself; then maybe I'll feel more consistently content, never jealous, envious. Grown up, working a job apart from the tumultuous arts world. I still find myself doodling those eyes in the night, when my catless, wifiless apartment grows too quiet, too dark, too lonely. And I won't lie: I tried to find amber lying around among Charlotte's magic rock collection, thinking maybe this would be a sign she's with me on your eye color, but alas.

- Now, don't get upset about this one. Apart from the borrowed stone and the photograph, really I'm just taking back what's mine. Right? My scent, my record, my drawing. The book was an accident. And I couldn't return the wand after using it. I know this one will get you angry, and I know you must know already. But as I was packing my car to go home, Nelly hopped in my backseat, just like old times. Maybe she hoped I was heading off for my next adventure, could probably tell soon it'd be back to the three of you again, a return to a dry domesticity. I couldn't say no, and she's half mine. She inspired me, truly, not to go back to my apartment, but to hit the road and start fresh, two ladies who've had enough of trying for you. Well, me, at least. Nelly would do anything for you. She sends her love. But we both feel voiceless, I think, incapable of being heard by you, maybe by anyone. From your book: "To have lost one's voice is not to keep silence: one keeps silence only when one can speak." No, I'm not silent. I just don't have a voice here. And, for Charlotte, I left a couple of shirts for her to wear awhile. When she gets a chance, I ask that she send them back my way. I think I really grew to love her again while housesitting for you. I love her for painting things purple, for finding power in pebbles. Tell her that, please. Thank you for a chance to reunite with my old lives. Will write with a PO Box number. Remember us. Remember that forgetfulness is "an act. I keep the memory at arm's length, as I look past a person whom I do not wish to see." Remember us, even if you remember us at arm's length. Remember yourself, too.

[contributor bios]

Heather Cripps is from Derby, England and has an MA in Creative Writing from the University of Kent. She has previously been published in *Forge Literary Magazine*, *Ellipsis*, *The Drum*, and more. In 2019 her novel in progress Beau is Fine was shortlisted for the Curtis Brown First Novel Prize.

Lucy Duggan is a writer and translator based in rural Brandenburg, in eastern Germany. Currently, she is working on a queer family saga set in a ruined manor house. She is the author of *Tendrils* (Peer Press, 2014), a novel about long-lost enemies. Her work has appeared in *The Catweazle Magazine*, *The Spectacle*, and *The Washington Square Review*. She recently published a collection of micro-fiction, *Tiny Stories* (Bylo nebylo, 2019). Website: www.tinystori.es.

Pearl A. Griffin is a writer and teacher from Vancouver, Washington. She holds an MFA in fiction from the Pan-European program at Cedar Crest College as well as a BA in English Education from Central Washington University. Her writing draws from a deep love of travel, an ever-increasing feminist perspective, and a personal history of hardship. You can find her work in *Gone Lawn* and *The Conium Review*.

[contributor bios]

Kelly Hill holds an MFA in Fiction and is a PhD candidate at the University of Louisville. When she's not writing or reading, she can be found spending time with her two teenagers, who remain unconvinced being a writer is a cool job.

Trista Hurley-Waxali just finished a stint living in LA for six years and is enjoying her new adventure living in the South of France. She has performed at Avenue 50, Stories Bookstore and internationally at O'bheal Poetry Series in Cork, Ireland and a TransLate Night show from Helsinki Poetry Connection. She writes weird short stories and is working on her novel, *At This Juncture*.

Kanya Kanchana is a poet and writer from India. Her flash fiction has appeared in Litro and Paper Darts. Her poetry has appeared in *POETRY*, *Anomaly*, *Asymptote*, *The Common*, and elsewhere, and translations have appeared in *Exchanges*, *Asymptote*, *Waxwing*, *Circumference*, *Aldus*, and *Muse India*.

Juliana Lamy is a Florida-based fiction writer with a Bachelor's degree in History & Literature from Harvard University.

[contributor bios]

Cassidy McCants is from Tulsa, Oklahoma. She received her BA in creative writing from University of Arkansas and her MFA in fiction writing at Vermont College of Fine Arts. She's the creator/editor of *Apple in the Dark* and is an associate editor for *Nimrod Journal*. Her work has appeared in or is forthcoming from *The Lascaux Review, Liars' League NYC, Gravel, The Idle Class, filling Station, Witch Craft Magazine*, and other publications, and her stories have received honorable mentions from Glimmer Train Press. She's a 2020 Artist Inc. fellow.

Erin Piasecki is a Graduate Teaching Assistant at the University of Nevada, Las Vegas and Design Assistant at *The Believer*. Born in Fredericksburg but raised in Albuquerque, she returned to Virginia to receive her B.A. in Theatre from the University of Richmond. She has work out now in *The Adroit Journal* and is currently working on her first novel.

[contributor bios]

Devin Porter is a New York based playwright, poet, fiction writer, and dramaturg. Devin uses his writing to grant voice to the ones who aren't heard. Born and raised on Long Island, Devin expresses his own individuality and unique style similar to his home state. His works analyze and examine the areas of race, political ideals, social class, and identity. Devin graduated with honor distinctions from the University of Albany with a B.A in English, where he was a three-time Spellman Academic Award winner.

Xenia Taiga lives in southern China with a cockatiel, a turtle, and an Englishman. Her work has been nominated for the Pushcart Prize, Best Small Fictions, and is part of Best Microfiction 2019 Anthology. Her website is http://xeniataiga.com. Her abstract artwork is available on Etsy.

Miranda Williams is a student and writer from New Mexico who currently resides in Arizona. She received her BA in Literature from Arizona State University in 2020 and is now pursuing an MA in Women's Literature. Her work appears in *Breakwater Review*, *Third Point Press*, and *Menacing Hedge*, among others.

9 781942 387169